新編保險英語

袁建華 ○ 編著

財經錢線

前　言

本教材在編寫過程中，參考了2005年由西南財經大學出版社出版的《保險英語》、2007年由西南財經大學出版社出版的 *General Insurance*。還特別參考了英國特許保險學會針對海外保險公司學員編寫的CII資格考試學習教材 *Risk and Insurance 510*、*Contract Law and Insurance 520* 以及本人在英國學習期間收集的保險資料。在此基礎上對篇幅進行了壓縮，修改了書中的一些錯誤，更新了最新數據，包括2009年修訂的《中華人民共和國保險法》、中國保險市場主體最新數據以及英國保險市場主體最新數據。全書共8章，內容更加精煉，層次更加分明，結構更加合理。

值得一提的是，經過10多年的保險教學，本人對保險理論和實務的理解得到了巨大的提升。因此，無論是課后的專業術語翻譯還是句子難點的翻譯，都比以前翻譯得更加準確、更加到位。本書最大的亮點是每章配備了幾幅與課文內容相結合的簡筆畫，由廣東金融學院保險系畢業生鮑汀元和勞動經濟與人力資源管理系畢業生杜斯帆同學根據本人提出的構思共同創作而成，增加了內容的趣味性和幽默感。

本教材共8章，內容包括風險與保險、保險與保險的職能、保險的四大原則、英國保險市場、保險公司的組織形式。為了讓學生更容易理解，每章課后編排了專業術語翻譯、難句翻譯、課后練習等內容。學生通過對本課程的學習，能提高閱讀金融與保險英文原著的能力，為未來的學習與工作打下堅實的基礎。

本教材是金融保險專業學生的必讀教材，可作為涉外保險業務工作者的培訓教材、各保險公司高層次專業人員出國前進行培訓的教材和進行專業英語選拔考試的參考教材，同時也適合各高等院校英語專業的學生和熱愛保險的學生自學之用。

由於編者水平有限，書中難免有不妥之處，希望使用本書的教師和學生以及廣大讀者提出寶貴意見，以便以后再版時修訂。

袁建華

目　　錄

Chapter 1　Risk and Insurance ……………………………………………（1）

　　Section 1　The concept of risk ………………………………………（3）
　　Section 2　The concept of insurance …………………………………（6）
　　Section 3　The classification of insurance ……………………………（9）

Chapter 2　The Basic Principle of Insurance（Ⅰ）- Insurable Interest
　　……………………………………………………………………………（23）

　　Section 1　The definition of insurable interest ………………………（25）
　　Section 2　The application of insurable interest ……………………（26）
　　Section 3　When insurable interest must exist ………………………（28）
　　Section 4　Common features of insurable interest …………………（29）

Chapter 3　The Basic Principle of Insurance（Ⅱ）- Utmost Good Faith
　　……………………………………………………………………………（39）

　　Section 1　Definition of Utmost Good Faith …………………………（41）
　　Section 2　Duration of the duty of disclosure ………………………（43）
　　Section 3　Representations and warranties …………………………（44）
　　Section 4　Breach of the principle of Utmost Good Faith …………（45）
　　Section 5　Remedies for breach of Utmost Good Faith ……………（47）

Chapter 4　The Basic Principle of Insurance（Ⅲ）- Proximate Cause
　　……………………………………………………………………………（57）

　　Section 1　Definition of proximate cause ……………………………（59）
　　Section 2　Analysis of proximate cause ………………………………（60）
　　Section 3　Modification of proximate cause …………………………（62）

Chapter 5　The Basic Principle of Insurance（Ⅳ）- Indemnity ……（71）

　　Section 1　Definition of indemnity ……………………………………（73）

Section 2　Concept of subrogation ……………………………………（77）
Section 3　Concept of contribution ……………………………………（79）

Chapter 6　Insurance Contract ……………………………………（89）

Section 1　Definition of general contract ……………………………（91）
Section 2　Definition of insurance contract …………………………（93）
Section 3　The contents of insurance contract ……………………（95）
Section 4　The conclusion of insurance contract …………………（96）

Chapter 7　Insurance Market ……………………………………（107）

Section 1　Concept of London insurance market …………………（109）
Section 2　London insurance companies ……………………………（110）
Section 3　London insurance organizations …………………………（112）
Section 4　Lloyd's Market ………………………………………………（115）
Section 5　Insurance intermediaries ……………………………………（117）

Chapter 8　Structure of Insurance Company ……………………（131）

Section 1　Structure of insurance company in China ……………（133）
Section 2　Forms of insurance company in foreign countries ……（137）
Section 3　Insurance companies as financial institutions …………（138）
Section 4　Types of insurance company organizations ……………（140）

Appendix I　OCEAN MARINE CARGO CLAUSES（1/1/1981）
………………………………………………………………（151）

Appendix II　Insurance Law of the People's Republic of China in 2009
（Amended）……………………………………………（155）

Reference Books ……………………………………………………（192）

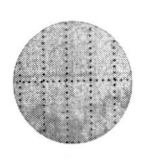

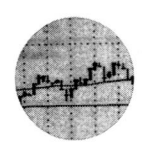

Chapter 1 Risk and Insurance

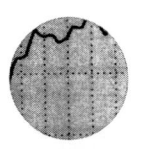

LEARNING OBJECTIVES：

☞ Understanding the meaning of risk
☞ Telling the difference between peril and hazard
☞ Understanding the concept of insurance
☞ Learning about the types of insurance

CONTENTS OF THIS CHAPTER：

☞ Section 1：The concept of risk
☞ Section 2：The concept of insurance
☞ Section 3：The classification of insurance

Where there is risk, there is insurance. In other words, without risk, there is no insurance. Only when we know what risk really is, can we know what insurance is. When we are aware of the existence of risk, we want to know what insurance can do to help us prevent, control and reduce the risk.

Section 1　The concept of risk

1.1　The definition of risk

When we use the word「risk」, we mean it will possibly cause losses or damages to someone when it happens. The outcome may be serious. In this way, we can say fire is a risk, theft is a risk, and personal injury is a risk and so on. What is the meaning of risk?

Risk can be defined as the possibility or uncertainty of damage and loss, but not the damage and loss that have occurred on a certain property.[1]

Risk is the possibility of an unfortunate occurrence.

Risk is a combination of hazards. Risk is unpredictable, which refers that the actual results may differ from predicted results.[2]

After studying the definitions, we know that there does seem to emerge some kind of common thread running through each of them. First of all, it has an underlying idea of uncertainty that we refer to as doubt about the future.[3] Secondly, it implicates that there are different levels or degrees of risk. Thirdly, it underlies the idea of a result which has been brought by a cause or causes.

1.1.1　The cases of uncertainty of risk

Suppose a child is playing basketball in the middle of a busy street; what will happen to him? If a worker is using a machine while he does not know that it is faulty and dangerous, what will happen to him? And if a pedestrian does not know the wall running alongside a pavement is dangerous and is about to collapse because of continuous rain, what will happen to him? There is an element of risk and uncertainty in the three examples. The child may escape free of injury, but he can be hit by a car. The machine may suddenly collapse and hit the worker. If he is lucky, the machine may hold out and does not explode until he has finished using it. And if the wall suddenly collapses, it can hit the pedestrian. If he is quick enough, he may escape from the falling wall.

In a word, it all depends on luckiness and fortune in above cases. We can conclude that uncertainty is not dependent on whether you recognize it or not. It always exists around us.[4]

1.1.2 Relations between Peril and hazard

Peril means the possibility that something is likely to cause injury, pain, harm, or loss and damage.[5] It is a risk accident. Hazard means something that increases the possibility of a loss. It is a factor that influences the outcome.

When a house is located on the riverbank, it will face the risk of flood. The risk of flood does not really make sense; what we mean is the risk of flood damage. Flood is the cause of the loss and the fact that one of the houses was right on the bank of the river influences the outcome.

Hazards are not themselves the cause of the loss, but they can increase or decrease the effect if a peril operates. The consideration of hazard is important when an insurance company is deciding whether or not it should insure some risk and what premium to charge.

We can conclude that flood is the peril and the proximity of the house to the river is the hazard. The peril is the prime cause. Often it is beyond the control of anyone who may be involved. In this way, we can say that the storm, fire, theft, motor accident and explosion are all perils.

Hazard can be physical or moral. Physical hazard relates to the physical characteristics of the risk, such as the nature of construction of a building, security protection at a shop or factory, or the proximity of houses to a riverbank. Moral hazard is a situation in which a party is more likely to take risks because the costs that could result will not be borne by the party taking the risk. In other words, it is a tendency to be more willing to take a risk, knowing that the potential costs or burdens of taking such risk will be borne by others. Therefore moral hazard concerns the human aspects which may influence the outcome. This usually refers to the attitude of the insured person.

1.2 The Classification of Risk

1.2.1 Financial and non-financial risk

A financial risk is one where the result or the outcome can be measured by money. For example, material damage to property, theft of property, house being damaged because of a fire, etc. All of them belong to financial risks. In case of the risk of personal injury, it can also be possible to measure the financial loss in the court by the judge awarding damages to the insured or make the settlement of the financial loss by negotiating between lawyers and insurers.

Non-financial risk would refer to anything that is not monetary or that which cannot be associated or viewed in terms of money.[6] For example, if you choose a new car from a car dealer, or select an item from a restaurant menu, we cannot say that they belong to financial risks. Other examples are the selection of your career, the choice of your marriage partner or spouse. All of these are non-financial risks because they cannot be measured by money.

1.2.2 Pure and speculative risk

1.2.2.1 Pure risk

Pure risk refers loss or a break-even situation. There is no chance of gaining profits.[7] The outcome is unfavorable to us or leaves us in the same position as we enjoy before the event occurs. For example, machinery may break down and take some time to be repaired. More examples are the risk of a motor accident, fire at a company, theft of goods from the factory, or injury at work. They are all pure risks.

1.2.2.2 Speculative risk

Speculative risk refers to a loss, a break-even or the chance of gaining profits.[8] For example, when you invest money in stock and security market, you may result in a loss, or a beak-even, if you are lucky, you may have the chance of gaining profits in the investment. Another example is that the manufacturer who provides credit to customers can be a risky venture, the goods have been sold by him in the hope of gaining profits, but the client or the customer may not be able to pay for them and the result is a loss.

1.2.3 Fundamental and particular risks

1.2.3.1 Fundamental risks

Fundamental risks are those which arise from causes outside the control of any individual or even a group of individuals.[9] In addition, the effect of fundamental risk affects large number of people. This kind of classification includes earthquakes, floods, famine, volcanoes and other natural disasters. Besides, social changes, political interventions and war can be explained as fundamental risks.

1.2.3.2 Particular risks

Particular risks refer to personal risks. They are much more personal both in the cause and effect. This includes many of the risks we have already mentioned above such as fire, theft, injury and motor accidents. All of these risks arise from individual causes and affect individuals in their outcomes.

In the early part of 17th century, unemployment was regarded as a particular risk in USA; it was believed or implicated that being unemployed was the fault of individual himself. However, technological unemployment of eighties and nineties has changed that viewpoint because of the changes in industrial and commercial world. People no longer emphasized the fault of individual himself, but focused on the society as the reason for unemployment.

Section 2 The concept of insurance

2.1 The meaning of insurance

Insurance can be defined as the ⌈term used to refer to a commercial insurance transaction whereby an insurance applicant, as contracted, pays insurance premiums to the insurer, and the insurer bears an obligation to indemnify for property loss or damage caused by an occurrence of a possible event that is agreed upon in the contract, or to pay the insurance benefits when the insured person dies, is injured or disabled, suffers diseases or reaches the age or term agreed upon in the contract.①⌋[10] In simple words, an applicant or an insured pays the premiums to the insurance company; the insurer bears the liability to pay the claims or give the benefit under the terms of the insurance policy.

---

① Insurance Law of the People's Republic of China. http://www.npc.gov.cn/npc/xinwen/2009-02/28.

2.2 The function of insurance

2.2.1 Primary functions

2.2.1.1 Risk transfer

The primary function of insurance is to act as risk transfer mechanism. Think of a car owner. He has a car valued at $200,000. The car could be stolen, damaged in an accident or catch a fire. There could be an accident, resulting in serious injury to passengers or other people. How will the owner of the car cope with all of these potential risks and their financial loss? We know that the owner of the car can transfer the financial loss to the insurer, in return for paying a premium.

2.2.1.2 Financial indemnity and insurance benefit

The basic function of insurance is to provide financial indemnity and insurance benefit.[11] In property insurance, when a subject-matter of insurance is damaged and the loss occurs, the insurer will give indemnity to the insured under the insurance contract. In life insurance, when an insured person dies, suffer diseases, is disabled or reaches the age under the life contract, then the insurer will give insurance benefit to insured person or his beneficiary.

2.2.1.3 Creation of the common pool

In order to demonstrate the common pool, let us concentrate on the risk of the owner of a house being totally destroyed and say that there is a one in a thousand chance that will happen during the year. It has no great value that one house will be destroyed in every thousand houses. But if a large number of houses would be destroyed, it does begin to mean something. For example, if there were one thousand similar houses, then we could say that one of them will probably be destroyed during a year. On average, therefore, the expected total loss would amount to $60,000. Knowing this, the owners of one thousand houses could all contribute at least $60 into a common pool, and there would be enough to pay the one loss.

The insured's premium is received by the insurer into the pool or fund for the type of risk. By collecting premiums from all individuals and enterprises, insurers can spread the cost of the few losses among all the insureds.[12] The insurer takes the insurance premiums from many people and pays the losses of the few out of the pool. The premiums have to be enough to meet the total losses in any one-year and cover the other costs of operating the pool including the profit of the insurer. Even after taking all these costs into account, insurance is still an attractive business in the world.[13]

2.2.1.4　Equitable premiums

It is clear that there can be several of these pools, one for each type of risk. The people who have a house to insure would not contribute to the same pool as those insuring a car. Operating in this way allows an insurer to identify which types of insurance are profitable and which are not profitable.

Even when risks of a similar type are brought together in a common pool, they do not all represent the same degree of risk to the pool itself. So the insurer has to ensure that a fair premium is charged, which reflects the hazard and the value which the person or company brings to the pool. Besides, the premium must also be competitive. There is not just one insurer in the market place and hence competition enters into the calculation. If an insurer charges a premium that exceeds the one quoted by other insurers, then he may lose the business. If he charges too little, the contribution to the pool would be less than required and loss would be made.

The three functions are all interest-dependent. Insurance can provide risk transfer mechanism by means of a common pool and each insured pays an equitable premium.

2.2.2　Subsidiary functions

2.2.2.1　Loss prevention

When risks are proposed to an insurance company, they will carry out a survey in order to assess the degree of risk. They make recommendations as to reduce the possibility of the occurrence of loss. Preventing disasters and losses is the important aspect in the risk management. The insurance itself is also the important aspect of risk management. Insurer plays an active role in participating in the work of preventing disasters and losses with other related departments.

2.2.2.2　Investment of funds

When an insurance premium is received and put into the fund, claims will arise from a few weeks or months until several years. The insurer can make full use of the idle fund to invest in order to gain the best overall return. The insurer can use the fund to buy government security, stock, money market fund or invest it in the real estate.

2.3 The Role of Insurance

First of all, insurance can ensure the society to carry out the reproduction. By insurance, the risk can be transferred and the social reproduction can be ensured. Secondary, insurance can guarantee the insured to enjoy his financial interest. As long as the insured has taken out insurance, he can get financial indemnity or insurance benefits from insurance company if the damages or losses or injuries are covered by insurance policy. Thirdly, insurance can bring the stability to the society. When a disaster or accident happens, perhaps it will cause damages or losses to property and injuries or death to people. Insurer tries his best to pay claims to individuals or business units and protects their normal life. Therefore insurance stabilizes the society.

Section 3 The classification of insurance

As insurance has developed, the various types of cover have been grouped into several classes which have come about by practice within the insurance company offices. Insurance offices are generally split up into departments or sections, each of which will deal with types of risk which have an affiliation with each other. There is a very wide variety in the way in which companies organize their business, but the following divisions are very common.

3.1 Ordinary life assurance

Ordinary life insurance includes many kinds of assurances. Here are some of them in the following.

3.1.1 Term insurance

In United Kingdom of Great Britain, term life assurance is the oldest form of insurance and provides for payment of the sum insured on death.[14] If the life insured dies, the face amount of the policy money will be given to the beneficiary. If the life insured survives to the end of the term, then the cover ceases and no money is payable. Depending on the age of the life insured, this is a very cheap form of cover and would be suitable in the case of a young married man with medium income to low income who wants to provide a reasonable sum for his wife in the event of death. Such policies can be issued for a period as short as one year or can provide protection up to five, ten fifteen, or twenty years.

3.1.2 Personal accident insurance

The intention of the basic policy is to provide compensation in the event of an accident causing death or injury. Capital sums are paid in the event of death or certain specified injuries, such as the loss of limbs or sight.[15] The policy is usually extended to include a weekly benefit for up to 104 weeks, or compensation if the insured is temporarily totally disabled due to an accident and reduced weekly benefit if he is only partly disabled from carrying out his normal duties.

In addition to the purchase of personal accident insurance by individuals, it is also possible for companies to arrange cover on behalf of their employees. These arrangements made by employers on behalf of the employees are also called employer's liability and many organizations arrange group life insurance for their employees.

3.1.3 Group life insurance

Employers sometimes arrange special terms for life assurance for their employees, with the sum insured being payable in the event of death of an employee during his term of the scheme is open to all employees working on the beginning date, or the anniversary date in future years.

3.2 Property loss insurance

In a broad sense, property insurance refers to property loss insurance, liability insurance, credit insurance, bond insurance and agriculture insurance. In a narrow sense, property insurance refers to property loss insurance including ordinary property insurance, cargo transit insurance, construction insurance, etc. Some of them will be discussed in the following.

3.2.1 Motor vehicle insurance

Motor vehicle insurance is a kind of popular insurance, for there are so many motor vehicles in each city. And it is also the major source of premium income for each insurance company in the insurance market. The minimum requirement by law is to provide insurance in respect of legal liability to pay damages arising out of injury caused to any person. Motor vehicle insurance policies can cover the third party liability, and fire risk as well as theft risk.[16] The comprehensive policies provide cover as above and in addition including cover for accidental loss of, or damage to, the vehicle itself. This is most common form of insurance policy in the European countries.

3.2.2 Marine cargo transport insurance

Traditionally marine policies include three areas of risk: the hull, cargo and freight.[17] While hull and cargo are easy for all of you to understand, the word 「freight」 may not be quite clear to some of the students. Well, freight is the sum paid for transporting goods, or the hire of a ship. When goods are lost by marine perils, then freight, or part of it, is also lost. Therefore the freight also needs insurance protection. Freight can be classified into two kinds. One is the prepaid freight. The other is the freight paid on delivery or on arrival. Other kind of freight is partial prepaid freight and partial freight paid on delivery.

The risks against which these items are normally insured are collectively termed 「perils of the sea」. The perils of the sea can be classified into two kinds. One is the natural disasters or natural calamities. The other is the accident event.[18]

Natural calamities include atrocious weather, lightning, tsunami, earthquake or volcanic eruption, flood and disaster beyond manpower. Accident events include grounding, stranded, sunk, fire, violent pilferage, jettison, collision, missing, overturn and the careless, negligent and malicious act by captain or crew. In China, Marine cargo insurance can be divided into three kinds. They are basic, additional and special risks. The basic risks include Free from Particular Average, With Particular Average and All risks. Additional risks include General Additional Risks, Special Additional Risks and Specific Additional Risks.

3.2.3 Property insurance

There is a whole number of different ways in which property can be damaged. One need only think of a small factory unit to imagine all that can be damaged and all the ways in which damage can be sustained. Companies, hospitals, enterprises, schools and individuals need this kind of insurance. Fire and theft probably come to mind first, and then there are very many different forms of accident damage, such as glass, electronic equipment, furniture and so on. In China, property insurance can be divided into two kinds. One is the household property insurance. The other is the enterprises' property insurance. The household property insurance covers the bedclothes and dresses, furniture, house decoration, electric appliances, etc. The enterprises' property insurance covers houses, buildings as well as the affiliated facilities, machinery and equipment, etc.

3.3 Liability insurance

As we know, the liability insurance arises under specialist branches, such as motor, marine and aviation, and engineering insurances. It is necessary for us to get some idea of 「general liability」 and it includes employer's liability, public liability insurance, product liability insurance and professional indemnity liability insurances, etc.

3.3.1 Employer's liability insurance

Employer's liability insurance covers the injury or death of the employees during the work.[19] When an employer is held legally liable to pay damages to an injured employee or to the representatives of someone fatally injured, he can claim against his employers' liability policy which will provide him with exactly the same amount he himself must pay out. The policy will also pay certain expenses such as lawyer's fees or doctor's charges where an injured man has been medically examined The intention is to ensure that the employer does not suffer financially, but is compensated for any money he may have to pay in respect of a claim. The policy is restricted to damages payable in respect of injury and does not apply where property of an employee is damaged.

3.3.2 Public liability insurance

Public liability insurance covers the accident that causes injury or death of the customers when they are in the public places.[20] If a person or customer goes shopping in the supermarket and is injured because of the wet floor, if a football fan watches an important football match in stadium and is injured because of the crowded audience and if a couple see a film in a cinema is injured because of the collapse of the chair or the fire, the supermarket, the stadium or the cinema is liable for the injury of the persons in all these cases.

3.3.3 Product liability insurance

Product liability insurance covers the accident causing injury or death of the consumers when they use the product.[21] If a person is injured by any product that he purchase from the supermarket and he can show that the seller or in some cases the manufacturer, was to blame, he can make a claim to the related parties for damages. It was reported 10 years ago that in China, some products, for example, the water heater, caused death of the some consumers because of product defectiveness when they are taking bath in winter. And also some fruit juice jellies caused the death of a small baby due to the defective design or without the warning cautions to the parents.

3.3.4 Professional indemnity liability insurance

Professional indemnity liability insurance can arise when lawyers, accountants, doctors, insurance brokers and a whole range professional man, do or say something which results in others suffering from a loss or loss of a lawsuit.[22] For example, a lawyer may give advice carelessly resulting in a client losing money. That client would then be able to sue the lawyer for an amount equal to what he had lost. Therefore lawyer can buy professional indemnity liability insurance to meet the cost of any award against him.

3.3.5　Personal public liability insurance

It is known to all that each individual owes a duty to his neighbor not to cause them injury to their body or damage their property. Liability may arise out of ownership of a house, a pet, out of sporting activities or just in the simple act of crossing the road without looking ahead.[23] There was a case in UK (Clark V& Mrs. Shepstone, 1968) that Mrs. Shepstone stepped from the pavement without looking ahead and caused a motor cyclist to swerve. The motorbike crashed and the pillion passenger, Mr. Clark, suffered severe injury. He sued Mrs. Shepstone and eventually accepted £28,500 in compensation. In the absence of a personal public liability policy, Mrs. Shepstone would have been in serious financial difficulties.

Professional terms

insurance	保險
uncertainty	不確定性
peril	風險事故
hazard	風險因素
unpredictability	不可預測性
underlying idea	言下之意
premium	保險費
moral hazard	道德風險
potential risk	潛在風險
financial risk	財務風險
insured	被保險人
pure risk	純粹風險
break-even	收支平衡
speculative risk	投機風險
fundamental risks	基本風險
natural disaster	自然災害
political interventions	政治干涉
particular risks	特殊風險
technological unemployment	技術性失業
insurable	可以保險的

commercial insurance transaction	商業保險交易
insurance applicant	保險投保人
insurer	保險人
insurance benefit	保險給付
function of insurance	保險的功能
risk transfer mechanism	風險轉嫁機制
financial indemnity	經濟補償
property insurance	財產保險
subject-matter of insurance	保險標的
insurance contract	保險合同
life insurance	人壽保險
common pool	共同基金
idle fund	閒置資金
collect premiums	收取保費
spread the cost of the few losses	分散少數人的成本
attractive business	有吸引力的行業
fair and equitable premium	公平合理的保險費
charge premium	收取保險費
interest-dependent	利益相互依賴
subsidiary functions	附加功能
loss prevention	損失預防
make a survey	開展檢驗
assess the degree of risk	評估風險程度
risk management	風險管理
other related departments	其他相關部門
overall return	全部的回報
government security	政府債券
money market fund	貨幣市場基金
real estate	不動產，房地產
taken out insurance	購買保險
policy	保險單
stability to the society	社會的穩定
types of cover	承保的種類
ordinary life insurance	普通人壽保險
term life assurance	定期人壽保險
sum assured	保險金額

15

face amount of the policy money	保單面值
issue a policy	簽發一張保險單
capital sums	資本總額，保險金額
weekly benefit for up to 104 weeks	連續每週給付至104個星期為止
compensation	賠償
employer's liability	雇主責任保險
group life insurance	團體人壽保險
property loss insurance	財產損失保險
liability insurance	責任保險
credit insurance	信用保險
bond insurance	保證保險
agriculture insurance	農業保險
cargo transit insurance	貨物運輸保險
construction insurance	建築保險
motor vehicle insurance	機動車輛保險
third party liability	第三者責任保險
theft risk	盜竊保險
comprehensive policy	綜合保險
marine cargo transport insurance	海洋貨物運輸保險
hull insurance	船舶保險
freight insurance	運費保險
prepaid freight	預付運費
freight paid on delivery	到付運費
grounding	擱淺
stranded	觸礁
violent pilferage	暴力盜竊
jettison	投棄
collision	碰撞
missing	失蹤
overturn	傾覆
negligent and malicious act	疏忽和惡意行為
Free from Particular Average	平安險
With Particular Average	水漬險
All Risks	一切險
General Additional Risks	一般附加險
Special Additional Risks	特別附加險

Specific Additional Risks	特殊附加險
household property insurance	家庭財產保險
enterprise's property insurance	企業財產保險
affiliated facility	附屬設備

Notes to the chapter

1. Risk can be defined as the possibility or uncertainty of damage and loss, but not the damage and loss that have occurred on a certain property.

風險可定義為損失發生的可能性和不確定性，但不是某一財產已經發生了損失。

2. Risk is a combination of hazards. Risk is unpredictability, which refers that the actual results may differ from predicted results.

風險是危險因素的結合體。風險的不可預測是指實際結果與預測的結果不一樣。

3. It has an underlying idea of uncertainty that we refer to as doubt about the future.

言下之意是不確定性是我們所說的對未來的疑慮。

4. We can conclude that uncertainty is not dependent on whether you recognize it or not. It always exists around us.

我們能推斷不確定性不依賴於你是否承認。不確定性總是在我們身邊。

5. Peril means the possibility that something is likely to cause injury, pain, harm, or loss and damage.

風險事故是指某事物可能造成傷害、痛苦和損失的可能性。

6. Non-financial risk refers to anything that is not monetary or that which cannot be associated or viewed in terms of money.

非財務風險是指不與貨幣有關或不以貨幣衡量。

7. Pure risk refers loss or a break-even situation. There is no chance of gaining profits.

純粹風險是指可能造成損失或收支平衡，沒有機會獲取利潤。

8. Speculative risk refers to a loss, a break-even or the chance of gaining profits.

投機風險包括損失、收支平衡或有機會獲取利潤。

9. Fundamental risks are those which arise from causes outside the control of any one individual or even a group of individuals.

基本風險是指任何個人或團體無法控製的風險。

10. Insurance can be defined as the「term used to refer to a commercial insurance transaction whereby an insurance applicant, as contracted, pays insurance premiums to the insurer, and the insurer bears an obligation to indemnify for property loss or damage caused by an occurrence of a possible event that is agreed upon in the contract, or to pay the insurance benefits when the insured person dies, is injured or disabled, suffers diseases or reaches the

age or term agreed upon in the contract.」

保險可以定義為「投保人根據合同約定，向保險人支付保險費，保險人對於合同約定的可能發生的事故因其發生所造成的財產損失承擔賠償保險金責任，或者當被保險人死亡、傷殘、疾病或者達到合同約定的年齡、期限等條件時承擔給付保險金責任的商業保險行為」。

11. The basic function of insurance is to provide financial indemnity and insurance benefit.

保險的基本功能是提供經濟補償和保險給付。

12. By collecting premiums from all individuals and enterprises, insurers can spread the cost of the few losses among all the insureds.

保險人從個人和企業收集保險費，將少數人發生損失的成本分散到所有的被保險人當中。

13. Even after taking all these costs into account, insurance is still an attractive business in the world.

即使考慮所有的成本，保險在全球依然是很有吸引力的行業。

14. In United Kingdom of Great Britain, term life assurance is the oldest form of insurance and provides for payment of the sum insured on death.

在英國，定期人壽保險是最古老的保險形式，提供死亡保險給付金。

15. Capital sums are paid in the event of death or certain specified injuries, such as the loss of limbs or sight.

如發生死亡或特定的傷殘，比如失去肢體或喪失視力，保險人提供最高給付金總額。

16. Motor vehicle insurance policies can cover the third party liability, and fire risk as well as theft risk.

機動車輛保險單能夠承保第三者責任、火災風險以及盜竊風險。

17. Traditionally marine policies include three areas of risk: the hull, cargo and freight.

傳統的海上保險單包括三類風險：船舶、貨物以及運費。

18. The perils of the sea can be classified into two kinds. One is the natural disasters or natural calamities. The other is the accident event.

海上風險可分為兩類：一類是自然災害，另一類是意外事故。

19. Employer's liability insurance covers the injury or death of the employees during the work.

雇主責任保險承保雇員在受雇期間的傷殘或死亡。

20. Public liability insurance covers the accident that causes injury or death of the customers when they are in the public places.

公眾責任保險承保客戶在公共場所因意外事故造成的傷殘或死亡。

21. Product liability insurance covers the accident causing injury or death of the consumers when they use the product.

產品責任保險承保客戶使用產品時因意外事故造成的傷殘或死亡。

22. Professional indemnity liability insurance can arise when lawyers, accountants, doctors, insurance brokers and a whole range of professional men, do or say something which results in others suffering from a loss or loss of a lawsuit.

職業賠償責任保險承保律師、會計師、醫生、保險經紀人等專業人士因所作所為造成的他人的損失。

23. Liability may arise out of the ownership of a house, a pet, out of sporting activities or just in the simple act of crossing the road without looking ahead.

責任的發生包括因房屋的產權、寵物、戶外運動或者橫過馬路時沒有抬頭看前方產生的責任。

Exercises

I. Questions

1. Give the definition of risk.
2. Give examples to tell the difference between peril and hazard.
3. What is moral hazard?
4. Give examples to show that we are surrounded by risks.
5. Give the definition of insurance.
6. Tell the primary function of insurance.
7. Tell the subsidiary function of insurance.
8. Tell the role of insurance.

II. Find out a word in the text that matches the same explanation and write down the word on the right column

1. Something that is uncertain or causes one to feel uncertain
2. A person or organization covered by insurance
3. An amount to be paid for a contract of insurance
4. Not able to be predicted
5. A person or company that underwrites an insurance risk
6. (Of a boat, sailor, or sea creature) left aground on a shore

1. _____
2. _____
3. _____
4. _____
5. _____
6. _____

7. Throw or drop something from an aircraft or ship　　　7. _____

8. An instance of one moving object or person striking violently against another　　　8. _____

9. The state of being legally responsible for something　　　9. _____

10. A document detailing the terms and conditions of a contract of insurance　　　10. _____

III. True or false judgments

1. Without insurance, there is no risk.　　　( )

2. Uncertainty is not dependent on whether you recognize it or not. It always exists around us.　　　( )

3. Flood is the hazard and the proximity of the house to the river is the peril.　　　( )

4. The consideration of peril is important when an insurer decides whether or not it should insure some risk and what premium to charge.　　　( )

5. Pure risk refers loss or a break-even situation. There is chance of gaining profits.　　　( )

6. Speculative risk refers to a loss, a break-even or the chance of gaining profits.　　　( )

7. The primary function of insurance is to act as risk transfer mechanism.　　　( )

8. The basic function of insurance is to provide financial indemnity and investment.　　　( )

9. Insurance itself is also the important aspect of risk management.　　　( )

10. Motor vehicle insurance is very popular, for there are so many motor vehicles in each city.　　　( )

IV. Multiple choices

1. When we use the word _____, we mean it will possibly cause losses or damages to someone when it happens.

　　A.「risk」　　　B.「danger」　　　C.「peril」　　　D.「hazard」

2. Risk can be defined as the possibility or _____ of loss and damage, but not the damage and loss that have occurred on a certain property.

　　A. probability　　　　　　　　B. uncertainty
　　C. unpredictability　　　　　　D. impossibility

3. _____ means the possibility that something is likely to cause injury, pain, harm, or loss and damage.

　　A. Risk　　　B. Danger　　　C. Hazard　　　D. Peril

4. Risk is _____, which refers that the actual results may differ from predicted results.

  A. predictable   B. possible   C. impossible   D. unpredictable

5. Factors which may influence the outcome are referred to as _____.

  A. risk   B. hazard   C. peril   D. danger

6. The proximity of the house to the river is the _____.

  A. risk   B. hazard   C. peril   D. danger

7. We know that the owner of the car can transfer the financial consequences to the insurer, in return for paying _____.

  A. a commission   B. a premium   C. expenses   D. fees

8. _____ is a kind of popular insurance, for there are so many motor vehicles in each city. And it is also the major source of premium income in the insurance market.

  A. Motor vehicle insurance   B. Life insurance

  C. Cargo transit insurance   D. Glass insurance

9. _____ risk refers loss or a break-even situation. There is no chance of gaining profits.

  A. Particular   B. Pure   C. Speculative   D. Basic

10. A _____ risk is one where the result or the outcome can be measured by money.

  A. Particular   B. Pure   C. financial   D. economic

V. Translation from English to Chinese

1. If a child is playing in the middle of a busy road; if a workman is using a machine while he is unaware that it is faulty and dangerous; if a pedestrian is unaware that a wall running alongside a pavement is in a dangerous condition and about to collapse, what will happen to them? There is an element of risk and uncertainty in each of these situations. The child may escape free of injury, the machine may hold out until the workman has finished using it and the wall may not collapse and injure the passersby. Otherwise, there could be serious injury in each case.

2. It is known to all that each individual owes a duty to his neighbor not to cause them injury to their body or damage their property. Liability may arise out of tile ownership of a house, a pet, out of sporting activities or just in the simple act of crossing the road without looking ahead. There was a case in UK (Clark V& Mrs. Shepstone, 1968) that Mrs. Shepstone stepped from the pavement without looking ahead and caused a motor cyclist to swerve. The motorbike crashed and the pillion passenger, Mr. Clark, suffered severe injury. He sued Mrs. Shepstone and eventually accepted £ 28,500 in compensation. In the absence of a personal public liability policy, Mrs. Shepstone would have been in serious financial difficulties.

Ⅵ. Translation from Chinese to English

1. 風險是損失的不確定性，是損失的可能性。
2. 風險不可預測是指實際結果與預測的結果不一樣。
3. 洪水是危險事故，靠近河邊的房子是危險因素。
4. 風險因素本身不是損失的原因，但是能夠增加或減少風險的發生。
5. 物理風險因素是指與風險的物理特徵有關。
6. 道德風險是指某一方可能更願意去冒險，因為不用承擔因風險帶來的成本。
7. 哪裡有風險，哪裡就有保險。
8. 財務風險是指其結果能夠用貨幣計算的風險。

Ⅶ. Case analysis

1. Suppose you want to establish a small business. The business is about a small grocery, selling foodstuffs and various household supplies. Describe the ways in which risk may affect your business. How you deal with the business? Describe the pure risks and speculative risks.

2. There is a large multi-nation petroleum company. It spends a large sum of money each year on insurance premiums. Talk about the benefits for the company, for the community and for the government.

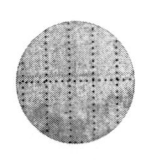

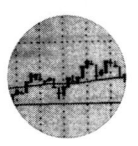

Chapter 2 The Basic Principle of Insurance(I)
– Insurable Interest

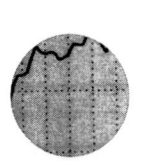

LEARNING OBJECTIVES:

☞ Understanding Insurable interest
☞ Learning about the application of insurable interest
☞ Learning about the common features of insurable interest

CONTENTS OF THIS CHAPTER:

☞ Section 1 The definition of insurable interest
☞ Section 2 The application of insurable interest
☞ Section 3 When insurable interest must exist
☞ Section 4 Common features of insurable interest

When we talk about insurance, we always talk about the insurable interest. Insurable interest is the basic requirement of a contract of insurance. The party to the insurance contract who is the insured or the policyholder must have particular relationship with the subject matter of insurance, whether it is a life or property or a liability to which he is exposed. The absence of the required relationship will render the contract illegal, void or simply unenforceable, depending on type of insurance.[1]

Section 1　The definition of insurable interest

Insurable interest can be defined in CII[①] textbook as the legal right to insure arising out of a financial relationship, recognized at law, between the insured and the subject matter of insurance.[2] Insurance Law of the People's Republic of China in 2009 (Article 12, Section I, Chapter II) states that the term 「insurable interest」 means the legally recognized interest that the proposer or insured has in the subject matter of insurance. Personal insurance is insurance under which the subject matter of insurance is the life and body of a person. Property insurance is insurance under which the subject matter of insurance is property and related interests therein[②].[3] The subject matter of the insurance refers to either to the property of the insured and related interests associated with, or to the life and body of the insured.

We can make a conclusion that there are at least four features essential to insurable interest. Firstly, there must be some property, right, interest, life, limb or potential liability capable of being insured. Secondly, such property, right, interest, etc must be the subject matter of insurance. Thirdly, the insured must stand in a relationship with the subject matter of insurance whereby he benefits from its safety, well-being or freedom from liability and would be prejudiced by its danger or the existence of liability.[4] And finally, the relationship between the insured and the subject matter of insurance must be recognized at law. The significance of insurable interest lies in the following:

---

①　CII: Chartered Insurance Institute. 英國特許保險學會。
②　http://www.gov.cn/flfg/2009-02/28/content_1246444.htm.

1.1 Avoiding gambling

In any insurance contract, the insured must have insurable interest to the subject matter of insurance. The law imposes the insurable interest on both parties (insurer and insured) to a certain subject matter of insurance in order to avoid gambling. There is an essentially difference between insurance and gambling. In insurance, the insured is immune from loss and his identity is known before the event. Insurer will indemnify him if a covered property is damaged or destroyed. Therefore he can restore his property and live in safety. In wagering, however, either party may win or loss and the loser cannot be identified until after the event. The winner is based on the cost of the loser.

1.2 Guarding against moral hazard

Moral hazard is a kind of artificial hazard. It concerns the human aspects that may influence the outcome. This usually refers to the attitude of the proposer or the insured person. If a person who has no insurable interest to the subject matter of insurance can obtain the indemnity from the insurer, he may intentionally make some artificial hazard.

1.3 Controlling the sum insured

The proposer's insurable interest to the subject matter of insurance is limited to the maximum sum insured.[5] In other words, the insured cannot obtain the excess payment from the insurer because of the accident loss of the subject matter of insurance.[6]

Section 2 The application of insurable interest

Insurable interest is applied differently to each of the main forms of insurance. It is important for the students to know these different applications in the following.

2.1 Life assurance

In life assurance, we can say everyone has unlimited insurable interest in his own life. The applicant has insurable interests over himself or herself, his spouse, his children and his parents. Other family members or close relatives, apart from the above mentioned, who have relations of fostering, supporting and maintaining with the applicant exist insurable interest.[7]

Notwithstanding the foregoing, with the consent of the insured to enter into a contract for the insured, the applicant shall be regarded as having an insurable interest on the insured. In theory, the applicant is entitled to buy a policy for any sum assured he wants, but in practice, the premium of the policy often limits a person's ability to insure his or her own life. A person who is married also has an insurable interest in the life of his or her spouse. Besides, a blood relationship does not imply an automatic insurable interest. For example, in Harse V. Pearl Life Assurance Co. (1904) in UK, an insurance policy by the plaintiff on the life of his mother was held to be illegal for lack of insurable interest, with the consequence that he could not recover the premiums which he had paid[1].[8] In the case, a son or a daughter cannot insure their parents' life, which is forbidden by law. In addition, certain people can insure the life of another person to whom they bear a relationship, recognized at law, to the extent of a possible financial loss. Accordingly, a creditor stands to lose money if the debtor dies before repaying the loan. Therefore an insurable interest is arisen to the extent of the loan plus interest.

2.2 Property insurance

In property insurance, insurable interest often arises out of ownership where the insured is the owner of the subject matter of insurance.[9] Therefore the houseowner can insure his house. A shopkeeper can insure his stock. In addition to ownership, some cases involve legal relationship and financial interest. For example, a joint owner having a partial interest in some property is entitled to insure to the full value of that property. If the insured property is destroyed, not only he and but also other owners will benefit all the amount of the claim payment, as he is regarded as a trustee for the other owners.

Another example is that mortgages, which are most common in the area of house purchase, involve the bank (mortgagee) and purchaser (mortgagor). Both of them have insurable interest. The purchaser is regarded as the owner of the

---

[1] Chris Parsons, David Green, Mike Mead. Contract Law and Insurance. Chartered Insurance Institute, 1995.

house and banks or a financial institution is look upon as the creditor. The interest of the mortgagee is limited to the amount of the loan. For example, if a house purchaser buys a house worthy of 600,000 Yuan, he pays his first sum accounting for 40 percent of the total amount. The insurable interest for the bank is 360,000 Yuan. Therefore the sum insured should be 360,000 Yuan plus the interest about five percent on yearly basis. Besides, the bank insists that the house should be insured by the mortgagor in the joint names of mortgagor and mortgagee.

In addition, a bailee is a person who legally holds the goods of another. These bailees including pawnbrokers, launderers and watch repairs are responsible to take reasonable care of the properties and to look after them just as their own. Therefore a bailee has insurable interest for these properties and he can buy insurance on his behalf.

2.3 Liability insurance

In liability insurance, a person has insurable interest to the extent of any potential legal liability he may incur by way of damages and other costs.[10] It could be said the extent of a person's interest in liability insurance is without limit. In fact this is so in a theoretical sense, but in a practical situation, liability to pay damages is based largely on legal precedents.[11] This means that whether a case is settled in or out of court, the damages awarded against the insured will be calculated according to similar claims settled by the court in the past. For example, claims for personal injury are different from claims for damages to property because the law cannot place a figure on the value of a particular injury that would be acceptable to everybody.[12] It is difficult for us to assess the value of the loss of an eye or an arm. Therefore any valuation is bound to be arbitrary.[13] The courts have designed a figure of compensation based on previous case law. This figure is not fixed in case of specific injuries being met, for example, 10,000 Yuan for an arm and 20,000 Yuan for an eye. The courts simply use previous cases as guidelines so that similar degrees of injury are awarded similar sums in damages.[14]

Section 3 When insurable interest must exist

The existence of insurable interest lies in different classes of insurance. There are some differences as to when the insurable interest exists.

3.1 Marine cargo insurance

In marine insurance contract, the insured must be interested in the subject matter insured at the time of loss, though he need not be necessarily interested when the insurance policy is issued by the insured. This follows from the customs of maritime trading that cargo may change ownership while it is in transit. The marine insurance policy is one of the essential documents in the transfer of title in such cases, and the buyer of goods is permitted to have a legitimate insurable interest in the goods from the time of transfer even though he did not have an interest when the policy was issued.[15] However, marine cargo insurance is different from life insurance. Insurable interest in life insurance is only required at inception. There is no requirement for insurable interest at the time of a claim.

3.2 Life insurance

In life insurance contract, insurable interest is only required by the insured at inception, not necessarily at the time of claim. The interest need only be valued at the beginning and there is no requirement for insurable interest when the beneficiary makes a claim to the insurer.

Section 4 Common features of insurable interest

Certain features of insurable interest are common to all forms of insurance. They are discussed below:

4.1 Insurer's insurable interest

Insurance companies have insurable interest in their liability to pay claims to insureds. This interest gives them the right to seek reinsurance. The purpose for the insurance companies to buy reinsurance is to satisfy the statute requirements, to spread risks arising from uncertainty regarding future claims experience, to obtain increased capacity, to finance new business, to improve financial efficiency, particularly in respect of insurance company taxation and to take advantage of wider range of services provided by the reinsurer. This performance by insurance companies still satisfies the principle of insurable interest.

4.2 Enforceable at law

Some people have certain legal right, but only an expectancy that those rights will materialize. For example, if a trader owns some property or goods and sells them, he has a legal right to any profits that the price may allow. He expects to make a profit if the property or goods remain undamaged. However, if the property or goods are destroyed, the expectancy to that legal right is defeated. This expectancy to profit is insurable because there is a legal right to the profits through the ownership of the property and the goods. Suppose an old man of ninety years old has an estate worth 20,000 pounds a year. Being incapable of making a will to his heir or inheritor because of incurable lunacy, no one will deny that his heir-at-law has moral certainty of succeeding to the estate.[16] Yet the law will not allow him to have any interest and he cannot arrange insurance for the estate. According to English law, the estate is only an expectation.

4.3 Possession

Lawful possession of property normally has insurable interest if that possession is accompanied by responsibility. For example, if you have purchased a house or a car with your own money, the house or the car is your property that is recognized at law. So you have insurable interest to the house or to the car. However, if you deliberately set fire to your own house or destroy the car, you will gain no benefit from the fire policy or motor policy if your criminal act comes to light.[17] A person cannot recover his indemnity under a policy in respect of his own criminal acts. But people can arrange insurance to meet the civil consequences of some breach of the criminal code. This happens often when drivers are found guilty of some road traffic offence and at the same time receives indemnity from insurers for damages to their own or another's property.

4.4 Financial valuation

Generally speaking, the amount of insurable interest must be capable of financial valuation.[18] This is straightforward in the case of insurance of property, liability and the rights interests. But in the case of one's own life or the life of a spouse, financial valuation is difficult because there is an unlimited interest in one's life.

With regard to other policies on the life of another, certain interests are capable of financial valuation. For example, the creditor's interest on the life of a debtor is the amount of the debts, plus interest and insurance premium. In other cases, for example, an employer in employee's life, the interest must be in a reasonable sense capable of financial valuation in money. In Hong Kong, the sum insured of an employee may be one million HK dollars.

4.5 Assignment of insurable interest

As we know, it is the interest of a person in the subject matter of insurance that is insured by the policy. Any assignment or transfer of that policy from one person to another will cause problems as the new holder of the policy may not have the same insurable interest.[19] Assignment of policy referring to transfer of rights can be carried out.[20] But in the case of personal contracts, such as fire or accident policies, it requires the consent of the insurer.

In general, assignment of personal contracts will only be valid with the consent of the insurers. Therefore policies covering property and liability are not freely assignable. In fact, when the insurer consents to the assignment of a policy, a new contract is concluded. The process of making such a new contract is called novation. We will discuss the topic of assignment in details in another chapter.

Professional terms

insurable interest	可保利益
Insurance Law of the People's Republic of China	《中華人民共和國保險法》
policyholder	保單持有人
blood relationship	血緣關係
unenforceable	不能強制執行的
legal right to insure	可保的法律權利
avoid gambling	預防賭博
artificial hazard	人為的風險因素
financial institution	金融機構

creditor　　　　債權人
debtor　　　　債務人
potential legal liability　　　潛在的法律責任
legal precedent　　　法律判例
out of court　　　法庭外
seek reinsurance　　　尋求再保險
satisfy the statute requirement　　　符合法定的要求
enforceable at law　　　法律可以強制執行的
expectancy　　　期望值
heir-at-law　　　法定繼承人
inheritor　　　繼承人
moral certainty　　　確實可靠性
lawful possession of property　　　對財產的法律佔有
assignment of insurable interest　　　保險利益的轉移
personal contract　　　個人合同

Notes to the chapter

1. The absence of the required relationship will render the contract illegal, void or simply unenforceable, depending on type of insurance.

根據保險的不同種類，缺乏所需的關係將會使合同非法、無效或者根本不能實施。

2. Insurable interest can be defined in CII textbook as the legal right to insure arising out of a financial relationship, recognized at law, between the insured and the subject matter of insurance.

英國特許保險學會編寫的教材對可保險利益進行了定義：保險利益是指被保險人與保險標的之間因經濟關係產生的合法權利，在法律上得到認可。

3. The term「insurable interest」means the legally recognized interest that the proposer or insured has in the subject matter of insurance. Personal insurance is insurance under which the subject matter of insurance is the life and body of a person. Property insurance is insurance under which the subject matter of insurance is property and related interests therein.

「保險利益」這一術語是指投保人或者被保險人對保險標的具有的法律上承認的利益。人身保險的投保人在保險合同訂立時，對被保險人應當具有保險利益。財產保險的被保險人在保險事故發生時，對保險標的應當具有保險利益。

4. Thirdly, the insured must stand in a relationship with the subject matter of insurance whereby he benefits from its safety, well-being or freedom from liability and would be prejudiced by its danger or the existence of liability.

第三，被保險人與保險標的必須處在緊密關係之中，即保險標的安全、完好無損或沒有發生責任事故，他就會從中受益；如果標的危險或存在責任事故，他將受到傷害。

5. The proposer's insurable interest to the subject matter of insurance is limited to the maximum sum insured.

投保人對保險標的的保險利益以最高保險金額為限。

6. The insured cannot obtain the excess payment from the insurer because of the accident loss of the subject matter of insurance.

被保險人不能因為保險標的發生事故而從保險人獲得超額的賠償。

7. Other family members or close relatives, apart from the above mentioned, who have relations of fostering, supporting and maintaining with the applicant exist insurable interest.

除了上述之外，其他家庭成員或近親屬與投保人有撫養、支撐和維持的關係的人具有保險利益。

8. In Harse V. Pearl Life Assurance Co. (1904) in UK, an insurance policy by the plaintiff on the life of his mother was held to be illegal for lack of insurable interest, with the consequence that he could not recover the premiums which he had paid.

1904年（英國），哈斯起訴明珠人壽保險公司一案中，法庭認為原告給他母親購買的人壽保險因缺乏保險利益而無效，他繳納的保險費也不能退回。

9. In property insurance, insurable interest often arises out of ownership where the insured is the owner of the subject matter of insurance.

在財產保險中，保險利益因所有權存在而產生。在所有權中，被保險人就是保險標的的業主。

10. In liability insurance, a person has insurable interest to the extent of any potential legal liability he may incur by way of damages and other costs.

在責任保險中，投保人的保險利益是發生損失和其他費用應承擔的潛在法律責任。

11. But in a practical situation, liability to pay damages is based largely on legal precedents.

但是在實際情況中，支付損失賠償費的責任主要是根據法律的判例來決定。

12. For example, claims for personal injury are different from claims for damages to property because the law cannot place a figure on the value of a particular injury that would be acceptable to everybody.

例如，人身傷害的索賠不同於財產損失的索賠，因為法律不能確定某一特定傷害的具體數額，讓每一個人都能夠接受。

13. It is difficult for us to assess the value of the loss of an eye or an arm. Therefore any valuation is bound to be arbitrary.

我們很難確定失去一只眼睛或一個胳臂的價值是多少。因此，任何評估都具有武

斷性。

14. This figure is not fixed in case of specific injuries being met, for example, 10,000 Yuan for an arm and 20,000 Yuan for an eye. The courts simply use previous cases as guidelines so that similar degrees of injury are awarded similar sums in damages.

這個數字不是固定在特定情況下遇到的傷害，例如，失去一個胳膊賠償一萬元，失去一只眼睛賠償兩萬元。法庭只是把以往的案例作為指導原則進行裁決，類似的傷害程度裁決以類似的金額作為賠償金。

15. This follows from the customs of maritime trading that cargo may change ownership while it is in transit. The marine insurance policy is one of the essential documents in the transfer of title in such cases, and the buyer of goods is permitted to have a legitimate insurable interest in the goods from the time of transfer even though he did not have an interest when the policy was issued.

根據海上運輸貿易的慣例，貨物在運輸期間可以變更所有權。海上保險單是產權轉移中最基本的文件之一。即使保險單簽發時，貨物的買主對貨物沒有保險利益，但是貨物的買主被容許對貨物進行轉移時，對貨物具有保險利益。

16. Being incapable of making a will to his heir or inheritor because of incurable lunacy, no one will deny that his heir-at-law has moral certainty of succeeding to the estate.

鑒於無法醫治的精神病而無法立遺囑，沒有人否認他的法定繼承人確實能繼承遺產。

17. However, if you deliberately set fire to your own house or destroy the car, you will gain no benefit from the fire policy or motor policy if your criminal act comes to light.

然而，如果你故意放火燒毀自己的房子，並且你的犯罪行為被發現，就不可能從火災保險單中得到利益。

18. Generally speaking, the amount of insurable interest must be capable of financial valuation.

一般來講，保險利益的金額必須通過財務評估。

19. Any assignment or transfer of that policy from one person to another will cause problems as the new holder of the policy may not have the same insurable interest.

保險單從一個人手中轉讓到另一個人手中可能造成許多問題，因為新的保單持有人可能沒有相同的保險利益。

20. Assignment of policy referring to transfer of rights can be carried out.

如果保險單轉讓指的是保險單權利的轉讓，那麼，是能夠進行的。

Exercises

I. Questions

1. Give the definition of insurable interest.
2. What are the four features essential to insurable interest?
3. Tell the difference between insurance and gambling.
4. Why can we say everyone has unlimited insurable interest in his own life?
5. What is the insurable interest in liability insurance?
6. Why do insurance companies seek reinsurance?
7. Why may any assignment or transfer of that policy from one person to another cause problems?
8. If a person who has no insurable interest to the subject matter of insurance can obtain the indemnity from the insurer, what would he possibly do?

II. Match up the explanations of the left column with the word on the right column.

1. A person or group in whose name an insurance policy is held
2. An organization founded for a religious, educational, professional, or social purpose
3. A person, country, or organization that owes money
4. (Of an insurer) transfer (all or part of a risk) to another insurer to provide protection against the risk of the first insurance
5. A person who inherits something; an heir
6. Play games of chance for money; bet
7. A person or company to whom money is owing
8. An earlier event or action that is regarded as an example or guide to be considered in subsequent similar circumstances
9. The state of thinking or hoping that something, especially something good, will happen
10. A body of people presided over by a judge, judges, or magistrate, and acting as a tribunal in civil and criminal cases

1. expectancy ( )
2. debtor ( )
3. policyholder ( )
4. precedent ( )
5. gambling ( )
6. institution ( )
7. creditor ( )
8. reinsurance ( )
9. court ( )
10. inheritor ( )

III. True or false judgments

1. Insurable interest is the basic requirement of a contract of insurance. （　）

2. Insurable interest can be defined as the legal right to insure arising out of a financial relationship, recognized at law, between the insured, the insurer and the subject matter of insurance. （　）

3. There are at least four features essential to insurable interest. （　）

4. The law imposes the insurable interest on both parties (insurer and insured) to a certain subject matter of insurance in order to avoid gambling. （　）

5. Moral hazard concerns the human aspects that may influence the outcome. This usually refers to the attitude of the insurer. （　）

6. Accordingly, a creditor stands to lose money if the debtor dies before repaying the loan. Therefore an insurable interest is arisen to the extent of the loan plus interest. （　）

7. Mortgagees and mortgagors both have insurable interest, the purchaser as the owner of the house and the building society or bank as the debtor. （　）

8. In marine insurance contract, the insured must be interested in the subject matter insured before the time of loss. （　）

9. In life assurance, insurable interest is only required at inception. The interest need only be valued at the beginning and so there is no requirement for insurable interest at the time of a claim. （　）

10. These bailees including pawnbrokers, launderers and watch repairs are not responsible to take reasonable care of the properties and not to look after them just as their own. （　）

IV. Multiple choices

1. Insurable interest is the legal right to insure arising out of a financial relationship, recognized at law, between _____ and the subject matter of insurance.

　　A. the insurer　　B. the insured　　C. the applicant　　D. the proposer

2. In property insurance, insurable interest often arises out of _____ where the insured is the owner of the subject matter of insurance.

　　A. ownership　　B. relationship　　C. property　　D. life

3. Another example is that mortgages, which are most common in the area of house purchase, involve the bank and purchaser. Here the bank is regarded as the _____.

　　A. mortgagor　　B. mortgagee　　C. mortgage　　D. debtor

4. In a practical situation, liability to pay damages is based largely on _____.

　　A. the requirement of the victim　　B. claims by the client

　　C. the calculation by the insurer　　D. legal precedents

5. In marine insurance contract, the insured must be interested in the subject matter

insured _____.

    A. at the time of loss   B. before the time of loss

    C. at the inception   D. at the beginning

6. Life insurance is different from marine insurance. Insurable interest in life insurance is only required _____.

    A. at the time of loss   B. after the time of loss

    C. at the inception   D. at the end of the loss

7. Insurance companies have insurable interest in their liability to pay claims to insureds. This interest gives them the right to seek _____.

    A. protection   B. reinsurance   C. insurance   D. prevention

8. However, if the property or goods are destroyed, the expectancy to that legal right is defeated. Therefore this expectancy to profit is _____.

    A. insurable   B. uninsurable   C. certain   D. uncertain

9. Lawful possession of property normally has insurable interest if that possession is accompanied by _____.

    A. interest   B. right   C. responsibility   D. capacity

10. In general, assignment of personal contracts will only be valid with the consent of the _____.

    A. insured   B. applicant   C. proposer   D. insurer

Ⅴ. Translation from English to Chinese

1. There are at least four features essential to insurable interest. Firstly, there must be some property, right, interest, life, limb or potential liability capable of being insured. Secondly, such property, right, interest, etc must be the subject matter of insurance. Thirdly, the insured must stand in a relationship with the subject matter of insurance whereby he benefits from its safety, well-being or freedom from liability and would be prejudiced by its danger or the existence of liability. And finally, the relationship between the insured and the subject matter of insurance must be recognized at law.

2. It is impossible to assess the value of the loss of an eye or an arm. Any valuation is bound to be arbitrary. The courts have designed a figure of compensation based on previous case law. This figure is not fixed in case of specific injuries being met, for example, 10,000 Yuan for an arm and 20,000 Yuan for an eye. The courts simply use previous cases as guidelines so that similar degrees of injury are awarded similar sums in damages.

Ⅵ. Translation from Chinese to English

1. 當我們談到保險的時候，我們經常談到可保利益。

2. 投保人對保險標的的保險利益只限於保險金額。

3. 在海上保險合同中，被保險人必須在損失發生時對保險標的具有保險利益。

4. 在人壽保險合同中，只要求被保險人在開始時具有保險利益。

5. 投保人對自己、配偶、孩子以及父母具有保險利益。

6. 保險公司對於向被保險人支付賠償的責任具有保險利益。

7. 在人壽保險中，只需要被保險人在投保時具有保險利益。

8. 一般來講，人身保險合同的轉讓只有徵得保險人的同意后才有效。

Ⅶ. **Case analysis**

1. A visitor came to Shanghai for sightseeing during a holiday. After he visited the Tower of Eastern Pearl, he went to the insurance company and made an offer that he wanted to pay premium to cover the Tower in order to protect the property. Do you think the local insurance company agrees to accept his offer?

2. Johnson is the owner of a house. The cost of rebuilding the house will be ￥600,000. He has a mortgage for ￥350,000 with Industrial & Commercial Bank of China. Discuss what extent both Johnson and Industrial & Commercial Bank of China have an insurable interest in the house?

Ⅷ. **Description with** 100~150 **words according to the picture below**

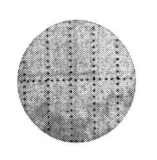

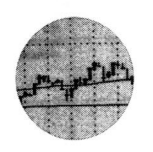

Chapter 3 The Basic Principle of Insurance (II) – Utmost Good Faith

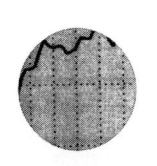

LEARNING OBJECTIVES:

☞ Understanding the meaning of utmost good faith
☞ Learning about the representation and guarantee
☞ Telling the difference between implied guarantee and express guarantee
☞ Learning about the misrepresentation and non-disclosure

CONTENTS OF THIS CHAPTER:

☞ Section 1 Definition of Utmost Good Faith
☞ Section 2 Duration of the duty of disclosure
☞ Section 3 Representations and warranties
☞ Section 4 Breach of the principle of Utmost Good Faith
☞ Section 5 Remedies for breach of Utmost Good Faith

Utmost good faith is very important in relation to insurance contracts. As you know, most commercial contracts are bond by good faith. These contracts are subject to relative laws. But basically it is the responsibility for each party to make sure that they make a good or reasonable bargain.[1] So long as one party does not mislead the other party and answers questions truthfully, there is no question of the other party avoiding the contract. It is unnecessary for one party to disclose information which is not asked for by the other party.[2]

In contrast to non-insurance contracts, insurance contracts put the proposer, in a sense, in a superior position. For example, the natures of subject matter of insurance, and the circumstances pertaining to it, are facts particularly within the knowledge of the insured.[3] The insurers are not generally aware of these facts unless the insured tells them.

While the proposer can examine a specimen of a policy before accepting its items, the insurer is at disadvantage, as he cannot examine all aspects of the proposed insurance that are material to him.[4] Only the proposer knows, or should know, all the relevant facts about the risk being proposed the underwriter can have a survey carried out, but he must rely on information given by the insured in order to assess those aspects of the risk that are not apparent at the time of survey. In order to make the situation more equitable, the law imposes a duty of Utmost Good Faith on both parties to an insurance contract.[5]

Section 1 Definition of Utmost Good Faith

What is Utmost Good Faith? Well, Utmost Good Faith can be defined in CII textbook as a positive duty to disclose, voluntarily, actually and fully, all facts material to the risk being proposed, whether the insured is asked for them or not.[6] Insurance Law of the People's Republic of China in 2009 (Article 5, Chapter I) states that the parties of insurance activities when exercising the rights and carrying out obligations shall abide by the principle of good faith.[7]

1.1 The duty of full disclosure by the insurer

As an insurer, he is also bound by this principle.

1.1.1 Disclosing information

He must not withhold information from the proposer, so as to lead him into a less favorable contract. For example, he must not withhold the information that the sprinkler system in the proposer's premises entitles him to a substantial discount on his fire insurance premium.

1.1.2 Unenforceable business

He should not accept an insurance business that he knows is unenforceable at law. For example, stolen motor vehicles and imported or exported goods without permission have no insurance interest. If insurer knows the information, he should refuse to underwrite them. Otherwise it is unenforceable at law.

1.1.3 Business underwriting

If an insurance company is prepared to set up during six months, he should not underwrite any insurance business.

1.1.4 True statement

He must not make untrue statements during negotiation for a contract.

1.2 The duty of full disclosure by the insured

Any material fact must be disclosed by the insured. The material fact means it would influence the insurer in accepting or declining a risk, or in fixing the premium or terms and conditions of the contract. [8]

Facts that must be disclosed are as follows:

Facts that show that particular risk being proposed is greater than would be expected from its nature or class;

External factors, which make the risk greater than normal;

Facts that would make the likely amount of loss greater than normally expected;

Previous losses and claims under other policies;

Previous declinature or adverse terms imposed on previous proposals by other insurers;

Facts restricting subrogation right due to the insured relieving third parties of liabilities;

Existence of other non-indemnity policies such as life and accident;

Full facts relating to and descriptions of the subject matter of insurance.

In fire insurance, the form of the construction of the building and the nature of its use must be disclosed. In theft insurance, the nature of stock and its value must be disclosed. In motor insurance, the fact that someone other than the insured will drive a vehicle regularly must be disclosed. In maritime cargo insurance, the fact that a particular consignment will be carried on deck must be disclosed.[9] In life assurance, the person must disclose previous medical history. In personal accident insurance, the proposer must disclose previous history which might make an accident more likely, the results more severe, or the recovery slower than normal.

Facts that need not be disclosed are as follows:

Facts of law;

Facts insurer should know;

Facts which lessen the risk;

Facts where insurer put on enquiry;

Facts a survey should have noted;

Facts covered by policy conditions;

Facts proposer does not know;

Spent convictions (Rehabilitation of Offenders Act 1974, UK).

Section 2 Duration of the duty of disclosure

The duration of the duty to disclose material facts varies from different circumstances.

2.1 Contractual duty

Sometimes the conditions of a policy state that the insured should fully disclose all material facts during the currency of the contract, and the insurer has the right to refuse to underwrite the change. In other cases, the policy condition may require disclosure of certain types of fact only.

2.2　Position at renewal

The duty of disclosure at time of renewal depends on the type of contract.[10] In long-term business including life assurance and permanent health, the assurer is obliged to accept the renewal premium if the assured wishes to continue the contract and there is no duty of disclosure operating at renewal. In other cases, renewal requires the assent or agreement of the insurer, and in such cases the original duty of disclosure is revised. The facts as applying at the time of negotiating the renewal must be disclosed.

2.3　Alterations to the contract

During the currency of the contract, if it is necessary for the insured to alter the terms of it, say, to increase the sum insured or to change the description of property insured, then there is a duty to disclose all material facts relating to the alteration.[11] This applies both to long-term and other business.

Section 3　Representations and warranties

It is very important for us to distinguish between these two classes of statement made in connection with forming a contract.

3.1　Representations

Written or oral statement made during the negotiations for a contract is called representations.[12] Some of these statements will be about material facts and others will not. Those material facts must be substantially true or true to the best knowledge or belief of the proposer. In many countries, insurance representations take the form of enquiry, questionnaire and so on. So does in China. Article 16, Insurance Law of the People's Republic of China in 2009 states that the insurer shall, prior to the conclusion of an insurance contract, explain the contract terms and conditions to the applicant and may inquire about the subject matter of insurance or person to be insured. The applicant should make a full and accurate disclosure.

3.2 Warranties

It should be noted that in ordinary commercial contracts, a warranty is a promise, subsidiary to the main contract, a breach of which would leave the aggrieved party with the right to sue for damages only.[13] However, warranties in insurance contracts are fundamental conditions that go to the root of the contract, and allow the aggrieved party to repudiate it.

A warranty is an undertaking or promise that something shall or shall not be done, or that a certain state of fact doses or does not exist.[14] For example, in fire insurance, the insured should promise that the rubbish is cleared up each night. In theft insurance, an alarm system is kept in good order under a contract of maintenance.

There are two kinds of warranties. One is express warranty. The other is implied warranty.

3.2.1 Express warranty

Warranties are usually expressed in the insurance contracts or written into it and must be strictly accurate. Even a slight deviations from the facts contained in the warranty will allow the aggrieved party the right to avoid the contract in law.

Warranties are often encompassed into the contract by a statement in the policy that proposal form is the basis of the contract, and on the proposal form there is a declaration by the insured that answers given are true to the best knowledge and belief.

3.2.2 Implied warranty

Generally speaking, warranties must be in written conditions of the contract. However, in marine insurance there are implied warranties or undertakings that the vessel is seaworthy and that the adventure is lawful.[15] In motor insurance, there is also an implied warranty that the vehicle should be roadworthy.

Section 4　Breach of the Principle of Utmost Good Faith

Breaches of utmost good faith arise either from misrepresentation or non-disclosure.

4.1 Misrepresentation

Misrepresentation is a false statement of facts that induces the other party to enter into the contract.[16] Fraudulent misrepresentation means a person knows that it is false. He has no belief in its truth and he does not make it recklessly. He does not care if it is true or false. An innocent misrepresentation is a false statement that the maker honestly believes to be true. And a negligent misrepresentation is also a false statement that the maker makes carelessly rather than dishonesty. Whether innocent or fraudulent, a misrepresentation must be substantially false; it must concern facts that are material to the assessment of the risk, or material to the benefits obtained by the proposer; it must have induced the recipient to enter into a contract of insurance. In UK, if a person knowingly, or recklessly to make misleading or false statements to induce someone to enter most long-term insurance contracts, he will be sentenced to seven years' imprisonment according to the Misrepresentation and Financial Services Act 1986.[17]

In China, Article 176, Insurance Law of the People's Republic of China in 2009 states that if a proposer, the insured or beneficiary commits any of the following acts and the insurance fraud activity engaged in by it/him/her is not sufficient to constitute a criminal offence, it/he/she shall be subjected to administrative penalties in accordance with the law:

The proposer deliberately creates a fictitious subject matter of insurance so as to fraudulently obtain insurance proceeds;

He/She fabricates an insured event that did not occur, or fabricates false reasons for an event or overstates the extent of the loss so as to fraudulently obtain insurance proceeds;

He/She willfully causes an insured event so as to fraudulently obtain insurance proceeds.

If an assessor, appraiser or attester of an insured event deliberately provides false supporting documentation to create the conditions for the proposer, the insured or the beneficiary to commit insurance fraud, it/he/she shall be penalized in accordance with the preceding paragraph.[18]

4.2　Non-disclosure

As a general rule, the parties to a contract are under no positive duty of disclosure. In some circumstances, however, a duty of disclosure exists. If a representation made in the course of negotiations subsequently becomes untrue because of a major change in circumstances, there is a duty to correct the original statement if the change takes place before the contract is concluded. But insurance contracts, the disclosure of material facts are so important that if one party does not disclose a fact within his knowledge, the fact that the other party does not know or the fact, if disclosed, which the other party does not want to enter the contract at all, then the other party can avoid the insurance contract.

Section 5　Remedies for breach of Utmost Good Faith

5.1　Options for the aggrieved party

The aggrieved party at least has three options for remedies.

At first, he can avoid the contract either by repudiating the contract from the beginning or avoiding liability for an individual claim.

Secondly, he can sue for damages as well, if concealment or fraudulent misrepresentation is involved.[19]

Finally, he can also choose to waive these rights and allow the contract to carry on unhindered. For example, if the insurer thinks that the breach of utmost good faith by the insured is insignificant, in the case of the insured not disclosing that the car is also driven by other person besides himself, the insurer can choose to give up his right not to avoid the contract.[20] It should be noted that the aggrieved party must exercise his option within a reasonable time of discovery of the breach, or it will be assumed that he has decided to waive his rights.

5.2　Exceptions for insurers

Certain insurances are compulsory. For example, third party liability in motor insurance is compulsory, which is required by statute. The purpose of these statutes tries to ensure that insurance payment will be available to the employer, the driver or the user to enable them to meet injury or property damage claims from third parties.[21] In UK, the Road Traffic Act 1972 prohibited the insurer from avoiding liability in the event of certain breaches of utmost good faith.[22] However, Insurers do endorse their policies to the effect that amounts paid in claims which would not have been paid, in the absence of statutory limitations, may be recovered from the insured.[23] The practical difficulties of recovering from an insured are so great that the insurers often do not enforce this right.

Professional terms

utmost good faith	最大誠信原則
insurance contract	保險合同
commercial contract	商業合同
good faith	誠信
make a good or reasonable bargain	做了一筆好的或合理的買賣
non-insurance contract	非保險合同
nature of subject matter of insurance	保險標的的特徵
disclosing information	披露信息
withhold information	保留信息
sprinkler system	自動灑水滅火系統
unenforceable business	法律無法強制執行的業務
business underwriting	業務承保
true statement	真實的表述
material fact	重要事實
external factor	外部因素
previous losses and claims	以往的損失與賠償
previous declinature or adverse terms	以往的拒保或不利的條款
subrogation right	代位追償權
non-indemnity policies	非補償保險單
spent conviction	已經過去的罪過
Rehabilitation of Offenders Act 1974	《1974年冒犯者改過自新法》
duration of the duty	職責期間
contractual duty	合同責任
position at renewal	續保時的情況
alterations to the contract	合同變更
long-term business	長期業務

permanent health	永久健康
renewal premium	續保保險費
representation	陳述
conclusion of an insurance contract	訂立保險合同
ordinary commercial contract	普通商業合同
express warranty	明示保證
implied warranty	默示保證
aggrieved party	受害方
seaworthy	適應海上航行
roadworthy	適應道路運輸
false statement of fact	事實的虛假表述
misrepresentation	誣告
innocent misrepresentation	非惡意虛假陳述
negligent misrepresentation	粗心大意的虛假陳述
fraudulent misrepresentation	詐欺性的虛假陳述
Misrepresentation and Financial Services Act 1986	《1986年誤告與金融服務法》
constitutes a crime	構成犯罪
criminal proceedings	刑事訴訟
administrative sanctions	行政處罰
options for remedy	補救選擇
avoid the contract	廢止保險合同
repudiate the contract	不履行合同
sue for damages	索要賠償金
waive right	放棄權利
exercise option	行使選擇權
breach of utmost good faith	違反最大誠信
in the absence of statutory limitations	缺乏法定限制

Notes to the chapter

1. But basically it is the responsibility for each party to make sure that they make a good or reasonable bargain.

但是從根本上說，雙方的職責是確保他們做了一筆好的或合理的買賣。

2. It is unnecessary for one party to disclose information which is not asked for by the other party.

如果另一方沒有詢問，一方無須披露信息。

3. For example, the natures of subject matter of insurance, and the circumstances pertaining to it, are facts particularly within the knowledge of the insured.

例如，保險標的的特徵以及相關的情況等事實，都掌握在被保險人手中。

4. While the proposer can examine a specimen of a policy before accepting its items, the insurer is at disadvantage, as he cannot examine all aspects of the proposed insurance that are material to him.

接受保險條件以前，投保人可以查驗保險單樣本。而保險人卻處於劣勢，因為他不能查驗對他來說非常重要的各個方面。

5. In order to make the situation more equitable, the law imposes a duty of Utmost Good Faith on both parties to an insurance contract.

為了使這種情況更加公平，法律要求保險合同雙方都遵循最大誠信原則。

6. Utmost Good Faith can be defined in CII textbook as a positive duty to disclose, voluntarily, actually and fully, all facts material to the risk being proposed, whether the insured is asked for them or not.

英國特許保險學會教科書把最大誠信原則定義為一種積極的職責，是指自願地、準確地、全面地公開（披露）所有投保風險的重要事實，這些風險不管保險人是否詢問，被保險人都必須公開。

7. Insurance Law of the People's Republic of China in 2009 (Article 5, Chapter I) states that the parties of insurance activities, when exercising the rights and carrying out obligations, shall abide by the principle of good faith.

《中華人民共和國保險法》第五條規定：保險活動當事人行使權利、履行義務應當遵循誠實信用原則。

8. Any material fact means it would influence the insurer in accepting or declining a risk, or in fixing the premium or terms and conditions of the contract.

重要的事實是指影響保險人接受風險或拒絕風險、確定保險費或合同的條件和條款。

9. In maritime cargo insurance, the fact that a particular consignment will be carried on deck must be disclosed.

在海上貨物保險中，裝運在甲板上的特定貨物的事實必須告知。

10. The duty of disclosure at time of renewal depends on the type of contract.

續保時是否告知根據不同的險種而定。

11. During the currency of the contract, if it is necessary for the insured to alter the terms of it, say, to increase the sum insured or to change the description of property insured, then there is a duty to disclose all material facts relating to the alteration.

合同期間，被保險人如有必要變更合同條款，比如增加或減少保險金額，或者變更被保險財產的特徵等，那麼有責任告知與變更有關的所有重要的事實。

12. Written or oral statement made during the negotiations for a contract is called representations.

合同談判期間所作的書面或者口頭的表述稱之為陳述。

13. It should be noted that in ordinary commercial contracts, a warranty is a promise, subsidiary to the main contract, a breach of which would leave the aggrieved party with the right to sue for damages only.

值得注意的是，普通商務合同中，保證只是一種許諾，附屬於主合同中。如有違反，受害方僅有權索賠損失費。

14. A warranty is an undertaking or promise that something shall or shall not be done, or that a certain state of fact doses or does not exist.

保證是一種許諾或承諾，許諾作為或不作為，某種事實是否存在。

15. However, in marine insurance there are implied warranties or undertakings that the vessel is seaworthy and that the adventure is lawful.

然而，海上保險中，默示保證是指（船舶）的適航保證和貨物的合法保證。

16. Misrepresentation is a false statement of facts that induces the other party to enter into the contract.

誤告是一種虛假的事實表述，誘導另一方締結合約。

17. In UK, if a person knowingly, or recklessly to make misleading or false statements to induce someone to enter most long-term insurance contracts, he will be sentenced to seven years' imprisonment according to the Misrepresentation and Financial Services Act 1986.

在英國，如果一個人明知或粗心地誤導或用虛假的表述引誘某人簽訂長期保險合同，根據英國《1986年誤告和金融服務法》條款，他將被判處7年監禁。

18. Article 176, Insurance Law of the People's Republic of China in 2009 states that if a proposer, the insured or beneficiary commits any of the following acts and the insurance fraud activity engaged in by it/him/her is not sufficient to constitute a criminal offence, it/he/she shall be subjected to administrative penalties in accordance with the law:

The proposer deliberately creates a fictitious subject matter of insurance so as to fraudulently obtain insurance proceeds;

He/She fabricates an insured event that did not occur, or fabricates false reasons for an event or overstates the extent of the loss so as to fraudulently obtain insurance proceeds;

He/She willfully causes an insured event so as to fraudulently obtain insurance proceeds.

If an assessor, appraiser or attester of an insured event deliberately provides false supporting documentation to create the conditions for the proposer, the insured or the beneficiary to commit insurance fraud, it/he/she shall be penalized in accordance with the preceding paragraph.

《中華人民共和國保險法》第一百七十六條規定：投保人、被保險人或者受益人

有下列行為之一，進行保險詐騙活動，尚不構成犯罪的，依法給予行政處罰：

（一）投保人故意虛構保險標的，騙取保險金的；

（二）編造未曾發生的保險事故，或者編造虛假的事故原因或者誇大損失程度，騙取保險金的；

（三）故意造成保險事故，騙取保險金的。

保險事故的鑒定人、評估人、證明人故意提供虛假的證明文件，為投保人、被保險人或者受益人進行保險詐騙提供條件的，依照前款規定給予處罰。

19. Secondly, he can sue for damages as well, if concealment or fraudulent misrepresentation is involved.

第二，如果涉及隱瞞或詐欺性誤告，同時他可以起訴要求賠償損失。

20. For example, if the insurer thinks that the breach of utmost good faith by the insured is insignificant, in the case of the insured not disclosing that the car is also driven by other person besides himself, the insurer can choose to give up his right not to avoid the contract.

例如，假如保險人認為被保險人違反最大誠信不是很嚴重，比如被保險人沒有告知，除他以外，還有其他人駕駛這輛車，保險人可以選擇放棄廢除合同的權利。

21. The purpose of these statutes tries to ensure that insurance payment will be available to the employer, the driver and the user to enable them to meet injury or property damage claims from third parties.

這些法規的目的是確保其雇主、司機和使用者獲得保險賠償金，以便支付對第三者的人身傷害或財產損失。

22. In UK, the Road Traffic Act 1972 prohibited the insurer from avoiding liability in the event of certain breaches of utmost good faith.

英國1972年頒布的《道路交通法》禁止保險人由於被保險人違反最大誠信的某些條款而免除賠償責任。

23. However, Insurers do endorse their policies to the effect that amounts paid in claims which would not have been paid, in the absence of statutory limitations, may be recovered from the insured.

然而，保險人的確背書了他們的保險單。假如沒有法定的限制，本來不應該支付（給第三者）的賠償金額也可以向被保險人提出賠償。

Exercises

I. Questions

1. Give the definition of utmost good faith.
2. What is material fact?
3. Give the definition of guarantee.

4. Tell the difference between implied guarantee and express guarantee.

5. What is representation?

6. What is fraudulent misrepresentation?

7. What is innocent misrepresentation?

8. What is negligent misrepresentation?

Ⅱ. **Find out a word in the text that means the same explanation and write down the word on the right column**

1. An agreement between two or more people or groups as to what each will do for the other 1. _____

2. Facts provided or learned about something or someone 2. _____

3. Substitution of one person or group by another in respect of debt or insurance claim, accompanied by the transfer of associated rights and duties 3. _____

4. A person who commits an illegal act 4. _____

5. A person's regular occupation, profession, or trade 5. _____

6. (Of a boat) in a good enough condition to sail on the sea 6. _____

7. (Of a motor vehicle or bicycle) fit to be used on the road 7. _____

8. An action or omission which constitutes an offence and is punishable by law 8. _____

9. A threatened penalty for disobeying a law or rule 9. _____

10. A person or organization that employs people 10. _____

Ⅲ. **True or false judgments**

1. Utmost good faith is very important in relation to insurance contracts.   (   )

2. In order to make the situation more equitable, the law imposes a duty of Utmost Good Faith on one of the parties to an insurance contract.   (   )

3. Utmost Good Faith can be defined as a positive duty to disclose, voluntarily actually and fully, all facts material to the risk being proposed, whether asked for them or not.
(   )

4. As for the insured, seven facts must be disclosed in the Utmost Good Faith. (   )

5. Sometimes the conditions of a policy state that the insured should fully disclose all material facts during the currency of the contract, and the insurer has the right to refuse to underwrite the change. (　　)

6. In short-term business including life assurance and permanent health, the assurer is obliged to accept the renewal premium if the assured wishes to continue the contract and there is no duty of disclosure operating at renewal. (　　)

7. During the currency of the contract, if it is necessary for the insured to alter the terms of it, say, to increase the sum insured or to change the description of property insured, then there is a duty to disclose all material facts relating to the alteration. (　　)

8. Written or oral statement made during the negotiations for a contract is called misrepresentations. (　　)

9. In many countries, insurance representations take the form of enquiry, questionnaire, roll and examination paper. (　　)

10. In insurance contracts, the disclosure of material facts are so important that if one party does not disclose a fact, then the other party can avoid the insurance contract.
(　　)

Ⅳ. Multiple choices

1. While the proposer can examine a specimen of a policy before accepting its items, the insurer is at _____, as he cannot examine all aspects of the proposed insurance that are material to him.

  A. advantage   B. disadvantage   C. benefit   D. non-benefit

2. _____ can be defined in CII textbook as a positive duty to disclose all material facts voluntarily actually and fully to the insurer whether the insured is asked for them or not.

  A. Indemnity   B. Proximate cause

  C. Contribution   D. Utmost Good Faith

3. For example, the sprinkler system in the proposer's premises entitles the insured to a substantial discount on his _____ insurance premium.

  A. fire   B. motor vehicle   C. marine   D. life

4. Facts that would make the likely amount of loss greater than normally expected _____.

  A. should be disclosed   B. needn't to be disclosed

  C. should be discovered   D. needn't discovered

5. Facts that are covered by policy conditions _____.

  A. should be disclosed   B. needn't to be disclosed

  C. should be discovered   D. needn't discovered

6. In _____ business including life assurance and permanent health, the insurer is o-

bliged to accept the renewal premium if the assured wishes to continue the contract.

    A. short-term   B. long-term   C. property   D. liability

7. Written or oral statement made by the insured during the negotiations for a contract is called _____.

    A. warranty   B. promise   C. representation   D. undertaking

8. A _____ is an undertaking or promise that something shall or shall not be done, or that a certain state of fact doses or does not exist.

    A. representation   B. contribution   C. indemnity   D. warranty

9. Generally speaking, warranties must be in written conditions of the contract. However, in marine insurance, seaworthiness of the vessel and the lawful adventure are two _____ warranties.

    A. implied   B. express   C. clear   D. underlying

10. A (An) _____ misrepresentation is a false statement that the maker honestly believes to be true.

    A. negligent   B. innocent   C. fraudulent   D. careless

Ⅴ. Translation from English to Chinese

1. Written or oral statement made during the negotiations for a contract is called representations. Some of these statements will be about material facts and others will not. Those material facts must be substantially true or true to the best knowledge or belief of the proposer. In many countries, insurance representations take the form of enquiry, questionnaire and so on.

2. It should be noted that in ordinary commercial contracts, a warranty is a promise, subsidiary to the main contract, a breach of which would leave the aggrieved party with the right to sue for damages only. However, warranties in insurance contracts are fundamental conditions that go to the root of the contract, and allow the aggrieved party to repudiate it.

A warranty is an undertaking or promise that something shall or shall not be done, or that a certain state of fact doses or does not exist. For example, in fire insurance, the insured should promise that the rubbish is cleared up each night. In theft insurance, an intruder alarm system is kept in good order under a contract of maintenance.

Ⅵ. Translation from Chinese to English

1. 不管是保險人還是被保險人，都受到最大誠信原則的約束。
2. 偷來的機動車輛以及沒有許可的進出口沒有保險利益。
3. 影響保險人做出決定的重要事實必須披露。
4. 火災保險中，建築物的結構以及特徵必告知。
5. 在人壽保險中，個人的醫療歷史必須告知。
6. 保險人應該知道的事實不必披露。

7. 誤告是對事實做出虛假的陳述，引誘另一方簽訂合同。

8. 向被保險人提出賠償的實際困難很大，因此保險人通常不行使這一權利。

Ⅶ. Case analysis

Mrs. Thomas decided to buy insurance for her household contents, including several items of jewelry under an「All Risk」section from Patrick Insurance Company. She completed a proposal form. From this document, the insurer assumed this to be a「standard risk」with no adverse features. They therefore issued a policy in their normal terms for this type of insurance and at their normal premium.

The insurance was renewed over the next few years and then Mr. Thomas submitted a claim in respect of several items of jewelry which had been stolen. On investigating the claim, the insurer discovered that Mrs. Thomas's husband had been to jail for crimes involving dishonesty, the crimes involved receiving stolen goods-cigarettes and spirits. According to this information, the insurer decided to refuse the claim.

Why do you think the insurance company refused the insured's claim when the insurer discovered the criminal record of her husband?

Do you think the insurer was justified in refusing the claim?

What do you think insurers can do or should do to prevent similar disputes arising in future?

Ⅷ. Description with 100~150 words according to the picture below

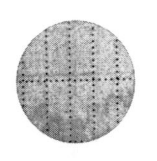

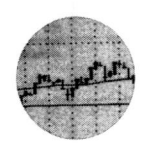

Chapter 4 The Basic Principle of Insurance(Ⅲ) – Proximate Cause

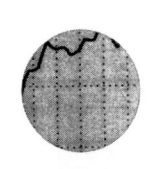

LEARNING OBJECTIVES:

☞ Understanding the meaning of proximate cause
☞ Learning about the application of proximate cause
☞ Learning about the modification of proximate cause

CONTENTS OF THIS CHAPTER:

☞ Section 1 Definition of proximate cause
☞ Section 2 Analysis of proximate cause
☞ Section 3 Modification of proximate cause

Every loss is caused by a certain cause. Some insurance policies cover a limited type of loss. Sometimes insurance policies cover many types of loss, but subject to various exceptions.[1] It is necessary for the insurer or the insured to examine the cause of the loss in details. Sometimes it is a single cause of loss, but sometimes there is a chain of causation or several causes operating concurrently.[2] The insurer should decide whether the loss is within the scope of the policy or not. We can find out the answer by studying the proximate cause.

Section 1 Definition of proximate cause

Proximate cause can be defined as active, efficient cause that sets a train of events in motion that brings about a result, without the intervention of any force started and working actively from a new and independent source.[3] Proximate cause is not necessary the first cause or the last cause, it is the dominant cause.

Stating that a cause is active and efficient means that there is a direct link between the cause and the result, and that cause is strong enough that in each stage of the events one can logically predict what the next event in the series will be, until the result takes place.[4] If there are several causes operating, the proximate one will be the dominant one or the most forceful one operating to bring a result.

1.1 Trains of event

Think of six dominoes standing on their ends so that the space between each is only about half the height of each domino.[5] If the top edge of domino one is tapped, this will cause it to fall against domino two, which in return will fall against domino three and so on. Until domino six falls down. Here there is a train of event bringing about a result. So the active, efficient cause which set it all in motion was the act of knocking over domino one.

If you had stopped domino 3 from touching domino 4, and then changed your mind and knocked over domino 4 yourself, the proximate cause of domino 6's falling would have been you. There would have been an intervention in the chain started by domino 1's fall and so it was no longer the proximate cause of the fall of domino 6.

1.2　Determination of the efficient cause

In practical situations, sometimes it is difficult to determine the efficient cause of a loss, as the volume of case law on the subject illustrates.[6]

Frequently, it is obvious what the initial event and the last event were. The difficulty arises in deciding if there is a direct chain of causation between them, or whether some new force has intervened to supersede the initial cause as the event bringing about the ultimate loss.

One method of coming to a decision is to start with the first event in the chain and ask oneself what is logically likely to happen next. If the answer leads one to the second event and this process is repeated until one reaches the final result, then the first event is the proximate cause of the past.[7]

Another method is to start at the loss and work backwards along the chain, asking oneself, at each stage,「why did this happen?」in an unbroken chain, one arrives back at the initial event.[8]

Section 2　Analysis of proximate cause

2.1　Storm

A big storm blew down the wall of timber building. This falling wall broke electrical wiring of the building. And the broken wiring short-circuited and sparked quickly.[9] The sparks cause a big fire in the timber building. The owner of the building called the fire brigade in order to save the building. They came to the building within several minutes and used water hoses to put out the fire and to cool neighboring building. Finally the water caused damage to the unburned contents of the timber building and to the neighboring buildings.

We can analyze and judge that there is a direct cause between the storms, the collapse of the wall, the fire damage and the water damage. You can imagine which cause is the proximate cause.

2.2　Earthquake

An earthquake overturned an oil stove of the house. The split oil caught fire from the burning wick. The burning oil set fire to the house. The first house, by radiated heat, set fire to a second house. Sparks and burning embers of the second house was blown quickly by a wind and set fire to a third house. Several more houses caught fire in the same ways. Finally, 300 meters away from the first fire, a house caught fire from its neighboring house.

We can analyze and make a judgment that there is a direct cause between the earthquake, the oil stove of the house, sparks and burning embers of the second house, the wind and the fire of the last house. You can imagine which cause is the proximate cause.

2.3 Fire

A fire left a wall standing but in a weakened condition.[10] Several days later, storm caused the collapse of the wall onto other property. A claim made by Mr. Gaskarth was refused by Law Union Insurance Company. The court decided that the fire was not the proximate cause. It was held that the storm was the proximate cause. The crucial factor was the delay of several days during which no steps were taken to shore up the weakened wall.[11] The chain had been broken. In UK, fire was covered and storm was not covered by fire insurance policy.

Another example is that lightning damaged a wall and left it weakened. Almost immediately afterwards, the storm blew the wall down. In this case, there was no time to take remedial action and the danger created by the lightning was still operating.[12] It was held that the lightning was the proximate cause. The author hopes the students can distinguish that the same lightning damaged the walls, but with different proximate cause.

2.4 Torpedo

It was wartime. A ship was hit by an enemy torpedo. The ship was badly holed and in danger of sinking. The captain succeeded in managing to reach a port. Repair work was started at once. Suddenly a storm blew up. The ship was still in danger of sinking. This risk was aggravated by the storm. In order to save the harbor from being blocked by the ship, the harbor master ordered the ship to leave the port. Finally the ship sank outside the harbor during the storm.

We can analyze and make a judgment that there is a direct cause between torpedo and the storm. Since the danger of sinking had never been removed, you can imagine which the proximate cause of the ship was.

2.5 Love affair

In 1970, a case occurred in UK. Gray had intimate affair with Mrs. Barr. Her husband, Barr thought one evening that his wife had gone to Gray's house, and he went there behind with a loaded shotgun. Barr did not believe Gray when he said that Mrs. Barr was not there, and he went upstairs to see for himself, firing a shot into the ceiling to frighten Gray. A scuffle broke out between them. During the fight, the gun went off and Gray was killed by Barr. Barr was accused of murder and manslaughter. Mrs. Gray sued Barr for compensation. The court thought that the proximate cause of Gray's death was his adultery with Mrs. Barr.[13] The judges could not agree on whether the first or second shot was the proximate cause of Barr's loss, nor on whether the cause was accidental or not. However, all four judges agreed that it would be against public liability insurance for him to be indemnified,[14] and so his claim failed.

The use of a gun is the crucial point here, since it is well established in law that one is entitled to an indemnity under the third party section of a motor policy for culpable manslaughter[①].[15]

Section 3 Modification of proximate cause

3.1 Policy wording

The perils relevant to insurance claim can be classified in the three types. Firstly, the insured perils: those named in the policy as insured, such as fire, lightning and explosion in the policy wording. Secondly, excluded perils, those stated in the policy as excluded, such as riot, earthquake, or war in the policy wording. And finally, the uninsured perils: those not mentioned at all in the policy. Storm, smoke and water are neither excluded nor mentioned as insured in a fire policy. We can see that there will be no insurance cover for the first event,

---

① Chris Parsons, David Green, Mike Mead. Contract Law and Insurance. Chartered Insurance Institute, 1995.

that is storm, but there may be covered for the second event, that is smoke and third event, that is water.[16]

3.2　Example of modification

Policy wordings dealing with exclusions sometimes exclude a peril if another one causes it directly or indirectly. For example, insurance wordings can exclude death directly or indirectly caused by war.[17] There was such a case in 1916. Coxe sued the Employers' Liability Assurance Corporation for indemnity. An army officer had a personal accident policy excluding death directly or indirectly due to war. In war time, he was walking along a railway line to inspect sentries who were posted along the railway line.[18] He was knocked down and killed by a train①. The proximate cause of his death was an accident but indirectly he was on the line because of the war. The policy did not cover his death. If there had been no war, he would not have been on the line, so that war was the cause of his death indirectly. Under the term of that policy, war, even as an indirect cause, the insured could not get indemnity from Employers' Liability Assurance Corporation.

Professional terms

proximate cause	近因
a certain cause	某一原因
subject to various exceptions	受到各種例外情況的限制
chain of causation	因果關係
within the scope of the policy	在保險單責任範圍之內
a train of events	一系列事件
intervention of any force	任何力量的干預
dominant cause	主因
practical situation	實際情況
efficient cause of a loss	損失發生的有效原因
work backwards along the chain	沿著因果鏈往后分析（推測）
initial event	最初的事件
timber building	木房子
fire brigade	消防隊

---

① Chris Parsons, David Green, Mike Mead. Contract Law and Insurance. Chartered Insurance Institute, 1995.

put out the fire　　撲滅大火
cool neighboring building　　使附近房屋降溫
unburned contents of the timber building　　木房子沒有燃燒的物品
oil stove　　油竈，油爐
split oil　　溢出的油，濺出來的油
burning wick　　燃燒的燈芯
sparks and burning embers　　火花和燃燒的余火
weakened condition　　不穩固的狀況
crucial factor　　關鍵的因素
shore up the weakened wall　　支撐不穩固的牆壁
take remedial action　　採取補救措施
intimate affair　　曖昧關係，風流韻事
a loaded shotgun　　裝滿子彈的獵槍
murder and manslaughter　　謀殺和過失殺人
third party section of a motor policy　　汽車保險單第三者責任一節
culpable manslaughter　　有罪的過失殺人
policy wording　　保險單的措辭和表達
perils relevant to insurance claim　　與保險索賠有關的風險
insured peril　　已保風險
excluded peril　　拒保風險
uninsured peril　　沒有承保的風險

Notes to the chapter

1. Sometimes insurance policies cover many types of loss, but subject to various exceptions.
有時候保險單承保許多種損失，但是受到各種例外情況的限制。

2. But sometimes there is a chain of causation or several causes operating concurrently.
但是有時候存在因果關係鏈，或者許多原因同時在起作用。

3. Proximate cause can be defined as active, efficient cause that sets a train of events in motion that brings about a result, without the intervention of any force started and working actively from a new and independent source.
近因可以定義為積極的有效的原因，使一系列事件產生作用，帶來一個結果。開始時沒有受到任何力量的干擾，從一個新的、單獨的源頭中主動地運轉。

4. Stating that a cause is active and efficient means that there is a direct link between the cause and the result, and that cause is strong enough that in each stage of the events one can

logically predict what the next event in the series will be, until the result takes place.

談到一個原因是積極的、有效的原因，是指在原因和結果中有直接的聯繫。這個原因很充足，人們能夠在事件的每一個階段從邏輯上預見在整個系列中下一個事件將會是什麼，直到結果產生。

5. Think of six dominoes standing on their ends so that the space between each is only about half the height of each domino.

想一想，把六塊多米諾骨牌豎立起來，每塊多米諾骨牌之間只間隔半塊骨牌高的距離。

6. In practical situations, sometimes it is difficult to determine the efficient cause of a loss, as the volume of case law on the subject illustrates.

實際情況中，很難判斷一個損失的原因，因為在這個問題上存在大量的案例法解釋。

7. One method of coming to a decision is to start with the first event in the chain and ask oneself what is logically likely to happen next. If the answer leads one to the second event and this process is repeated until one reaches the final result, then the first event is the proximate cause of the past.

確定近因的一種方法是從因果鏈中的第一個事件開始，然后問自己下一步邏輯上可能會發生什麼。如果這個回答能導出第二個事件，然后重複這一過程，直到這個原因產生最后的結果。那麼第一個事件就是過去的近因。

8. Another method is to start at a loss and work backwards along the chain, asking oneself, at each stage,「why did this happen?」in an unbroken chain, one arrives back at the initial event.

確定近因的另一種方法是從損失開始分析，然后沿著這個因果鏈往后分析推論，在每個階段問問自己，「為什麼這個發生了？」在不間斷的因果鏈中，由此而推論回到最初的事件。

9. And the broken wiring short-circuited and sparked quickly.

折斷的電線發生短路，迅速產生火花。

10. A fire left a wall standing but in a weakened condition.

火災發生后，牆壁還豎立著，但是處於不穩固的狀態。

11. The crucial factor was the delay of several days during which no steps were taken to shore up the weakened wall.

關鍵的因素是延誤了許多天，在這個期間，沒有採取措施，以支撐不牢固的牆壁。

12. There was no time to take remedial action and the danger created by the lightning was still operating.

沒有時間採取補救行動，雷電產生的危險依然在起作用。

13. The court thought that the proximate cause of Gray's death was his adultery with Mrs. Barr.

法庭認為，格雷死亡的近因是他與巴爾夫人通奸造成的。

14. However, all four judges agreed that it would be against public liability insurance for him to be indemnified.

然而，所有四個法官都一直認為，對他的賠償不符合公眾責任保險的條款。

15. The use of a gun is the crucial point here, since it is well established in law that one is entitled to an indemnity under the third party section of a motor policy for culpable manslaughter.

此時使用獵槍是關鍵的因素，因為法律已經確立，汽車保險單第三者責任一節中，對於有罪的過失殺人，（受害人）可以得到保險賠償。

16. Storm, smoke and water are neither excluded nor mentioned as insured in a fire policy. We can see that there will be no insurance cover for the first event, that is storm, but there may be covered for the second event, that is smoke and third event, that is water.

火災保險單中，暴風雨、菸霧和雨水既不是責任免除，也沒有提及是保險責任。我們知道，第一個事件，即暴風雨是不保的，而第二個事件，即菸霧是可以保險的，包括第三個事件，即雨水，也是可以保險的。

17. Policy wordings dealing with exclusions sometimes exclude a peril if another one causes it directly or indirectly. For example, insurance wordings can exclude death directly or indirectly caused by war.

涉及責任免除的保險單條款中，如果另一原因直接或間接起作用，那麼這個原因造成的風險有時候被認為是責任免除。

18. He was walking along a railway line to inspect sentries who were posted along the railway line.

他正沿著鐵路線行走，視察駐扎在鐵路沿線的士兵。

Exercises

I. Questions

1. Give the meaning of proximate cause.
2. How many methods are there in determining the proximate cause?
3. In practical situations, why is it difficult to determine the efficient cause of a loss?
4. What is the proximate cause in case of storm?
5. What is the proximate cause in case of earthquake?
6. What is the proximate cause in case of torpedo?

7. Why could not Barr's public liability insurance cover his manslaughter to Gray?

8. Why did the insurer refuse the claim when the officer was killed by the train?

II. **Match up the explanations of the left column with the word on the right column**

1. (Especially of the cause of something) closest in relationship; immediate
2. A person or thing that is excluded from a general statement or does not follow a rule
3. (Of a system or machine) achieving maximum productivity with minimum wasted effort or expense
4. Having power and influence over others
5. A structure with a roof and walls, such as a house or factory
6. Not covered by insurance
7. A smooth-bore gun for firing small shot at short range
8. A process in which substances combine chemically with oxygen from the air and give out bright light, heat, and smoke; or burning
9. A continuous vertical brick or stone structure that encloses or divides an area of land
10. The crime of killing a human being without malice aforethought, or in circumstances not amounting to murder

1. efficient (　)
2. dominant (　)
3. building (　)
4. exception (　)
5. fire (　)
6. wall (　)
7. manslaughter (　)
8. proximate (　)
9. uninsured (　)
10. shotgun (　)

III. **True or false judgments**

1. Proximate cause can be defined as active, efficient cause that sets a train of events in motion that brings about a result, with the intervention of any force started and working actively from a new and dependent source. (　)

2. In practical situations, sometimes it is easy to determine the efficient cause of a loss, as the volume of case law on the subject illustrates. (　)

3. Another method is to start at the loss and work backwards along the chain, asking oneself, at each stage,「why did this happen?」in an unbroken chain, one arrives back at the initial event. (　)

4. The court thought that the proximate cause of Gray's death was his adultery with Mrs. Barr.   (   )

5. The use of a gun is the crucial point here, since it is well established in law that one has no right to get indemnity under the third party section of a motor policy for culpable manslaughter.   (   )

6. Policy wordings dealing with exclusions sometimes exclude a peril if another one causes it directly or indirectly.   (   )

7. The officer's death was directly due to war. However, if there had been no war, he would not have been on the line, so that war was the direct cause of his death.   (   )

8. The crucial factor was the delay of several days during which no steps were taken to shore up the weakened wall.   (   )

9. Under the term of that policy, war, even as an indirect cause, the insured could get indemnity from Employers' Liability Assurance Corporation.   (   )

10. For example, if the building next door to the insured catches fire and the only damage that the insured suffers is by water or smoke, his fire policy will not cover the damage.
                                                                                                                                                    (   )

Ⅳ. Multiple choices

1. _____ is an active and efficient cause that sets a train of events in motion and brings about a result.

  A. Insurable interest   B. Proximate cause

  C. Subrogation   D. Contribution

2. Another method is to start at the loss and work backwards along the chain, asking oneself, at each stage, 「why did this happen?」in an unbroken chain, one arrives back at the _____ event.

  A. before B. last C. after D. initial

3. The crucial factor was the delay of several days during which no steps were taken to shore up the weakened wall.

  A. delay B. beginning C. work D. last

4. There was no time to take remedial action and the danger _____ by the lightning was still operating.

  A. made B. created C. done D. given

5. Storm, smoke and water are neither excluded nor mentioned as insured in a _____ policy.

  A. motor B. liability C. life D. fire policy

6. Policy wordings dealing with _____ sometimes exclude a peril if another one causes

it directly or indirectly.

    A. liability   B. obligations   C. except   D. exclusions

7. The perils relevant to insurance claim can be classified in the _____ types.

    A. five   B. three   C. four   D. six

8. The court thought that the _____ of Gray's death was his adultery with Mrs. Barr.

    A. major cause   B. proximate cause

    C. remote cause   D. main cause

9. The active, efficient cause which set it all in _____ was the act of knocking over domino one.

    A. movement   B. motion   C. motive   D. operation

10. The author hopes the students can distinguish from the same lightning that damaged the walls, but with _____ proximate cause.

    A. common   B. contrary   C. same   D. different

Ⅴ. Translation from English to Chinese

1. Think of six dominoes standing on their ends so that the space between each is only about half the height of each domino. If the top edge of domino one is tapped, this will cause it to fall against domino two, which in return will fall against domino three and so on. Until domino six falls down. Here there is a train of event bringing about a result. So the active, efficient cause which set it all in motion was the act of knocking over domino one.

2. In 1970, a case occurred in UK. Gray had intimate affair with Mrs. Barr. Her husband, Barr thought one evening that his wife had gone to Gray's house, and he went there behind with a loaded shotgun. Barr did not believe Gray when he said that Mrs. Barr was not there, and he went upstairs to see for himself, firing a shot into the ceiling to frighten Gray. A scuffle broke out between them. During the fight, the gun went off and Gray was killed by Barr. Barr was accused of murder and manslaughter. Mrs. Gray sued Barr for compensation. The court thought that the proximate cause of Gray's death was his adultery with Mrs. Barr. The judges could not agree on whether the first or second shot was the proximate cause of Barr's loss, nor on whether the cause was accidental or not. However, all four judges agreed that it would be against public liability insurance for him to be indemnified, and so his claim failed.

Ⅵ. Translation from Chinese to English

1. 與保險索賠有關的風險可分為三大類：第一類為被保風險；第二類為除外風險；第三類為沒有提到的風險。

2. 保險人和被保險人有必要仔細檢查損失的原因。

3. 判斷他們之間是否有直接的因果關係鏈有難度。

4. 在英國，火災保險單中，火災是保險的，而暴風雨是不保的。

5. 希望學生能夠區分同樣是雷電造成牆壁的損失，但是近因是不一樣的。

6. 法官不能確定是第一槍還是第二槍是近因造成巴爾的損失，也不能確定是否為意外事故。

7. 如果沒有戰爭，他不可能到鐵路沿線去。

Ⅶ. **Case analysis**

A theft policy excluded losses due to the war. During an enemy air raid one night, all the street lights were turned off in order not to illuminate targets for the enemy aircraft. Under cover of this blackout, a thief broke into a warehouse and stole some of the insured property.

Do you think the insurance company should pay the claim to the insured? Why?

Can the insurance company refuse the claim? Give the reasons.

Ⅷ. **Description with** 100~150 **words according to the picture below**

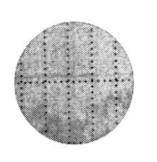

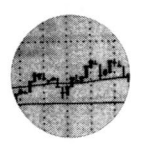

Chapter 5 The Basic Principle of Insurance (IV) – Indemnity

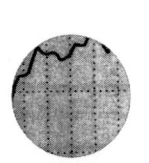

LEARNING OBJECTIVES:

☞ Understanding the meaning of indemnity
☞ Learning about the types of indemnity
☞ Learning about the ways of contribution

CONTENTS OF THIS CHAPTER:

☞ Section 1 Definition of indemnity
☞ Section 2 Concept of subrogation
☞ Section 3 Concept of contribution

Indemnity is one of the most important principles in insurance because the basic function of insurance is the financial compensation.[1] Most insurance contracts are contracts of indemnity except life insurance. In order to understand how it works, we will discuss indemnity as well as its derivative principle respectively: subrogation and contribution.

Section 1　Definition of indemnity

Indemnity in the property insurance contract can be defined as exact financial compensation. The indemnity should be sufficient to place the insured in the same financial position after a loss as he can enjoy the benefit before it occurs[①].[2] In other words, when claims occur in property insurance, the insurer will pay the claims to the insured if the loss or damage is covered by the policy conditions.

The principle of indemnity relies on financial evaluation. In life and personal accident insurance, there is an unlimited interest. So in life insurance, indemnity is impossible. Because life and personal accident policies are not contracts of indemnity, the value of a person's life or limb cannot be measured by money. But if it is a personal accident policy which is bought by an employer on his staff, the policy is intended to provide the employer with any amount he would have to pay to a sick employee for his wage.[3]

1.1　The ways of providing indemnity

When a valid claim arises, there are at least four methods that insurers can choose in providing indemnity.

1.1.1　Cash payment

In the vast majority of cases, the claim is settled by giving the insured the cash for the amount payable under the insurance policy. This is an old ways of payment. Nowadays electric payment is often used to settle the claims of payment.

1.1.2　Repair

Insurance companies make full use of repair as a method of providing indem-

---

① Chris Parsons. Contract Law and Insurance. Chartered Insurance Institute, 1995.

nity in motor insurance. Insurance companies often authorize certain car garages to carry out repair work on damaged vehicles so that the cost of repair will be more reasonable and cheap.[4]

In addition to the authorized garages, some big insurance companies set up their own car garages. For example, the insured can drive or have his car pulled into the insurer's garage, complete a claim form, have the vehicle examined and have the work carried out all in one roof.[5] It is very convenient for the both parties.

1.1.3 Replacement

In most cases, replacement refers to glass insurance. For example, broken windows and other items are replaced on behalf of insurers by glazing companies. Insurers can enjoy a discount from the glazing firms if insurers give vast amount of work for them.

1.1.4 Reinstatement

As a method of providing indemnity, it refers to property insurance and sometimes an insurance company promises to restore or rebuild a building damaged by fire. The insurance company can decide whether he pays money or provides a building. Insurance companies must restore the property substantially to the same condition as before the loss occurs.

1.2 Measurement of indemnity

The method by which indemnity is to be measured depends on the types of insurance.

1.2.1 Marine insurance

In marine insurance, there are two kinds of policies. One is unvalued policy. Another is valued policy. In a valued policy, the insurable value is agreed by two parties in advance. Therefore in each of the policies, there is a fixed insurable value which is operative from the beginning of the risk and is unaffected by subsequent market fluctuations.

In the event of total loss, the measurement of indemnity is the value fixed by the policy. If there is a partial loss of goods, a settlement is made of a proportion of the agreed value according to the amount of depreciation.[6] In the event of a partial loss of a ship, the indemnity is represented by the cost of repairing the damage.

1.2.2 Property insurance

In buildings, if the insured intends to repair or reinstate the property in its previous form. Then indemnity is the cost of that work less an allowance for depreciation as appropriate.[7] In practice, the indemnity sum for loss or damage to building can be calculated as the cost of repair or reconstruction at the time of loss, less an allowance for betterment.[8] Betterment can take two forms. Firstly, when property is repaired or replaced, certain aspects such as new plumbing, electrical wiring, etc. are perhaps in a better condition than before.

1.2.3 Pecuniary insurance

In guarantee policies, the measurement of indemnity is easy to ascertain. It is based on actual financial loss suffered by the insured as a result of the dishonest of a cashier. In business interruption insurance, it is a little more difficult to establish indemnity. But with the help of the insured's accountants, it is necessary to try to establish what profit the firm would have made if the fire or other insured peril had not occurred.

1.2.4 Liability insurance

Indemnity is easily established in liability insurance. It is the amount of any award made by the court or it is an out-of-court settlement by the negotiation between the two parties.[9]

1.3 Factors limiting the payment of indemnity

There are many factors restricting the insured to receive less than a full indemnity in the event of a claim. Several of them will be discussed below.

1.3.1 The sum insured

The maximum amount recoverable under any policy is limited by either the sum insured or the limit of indemnity.[10] The use of the phrase maximum amount recoverable does not imply that this is the amount payable to the insured. The actual amount is governed by a number of considerations. All that is implied here is that the sum insured is the maximum recoverable.

1.3.2 Average

In case of under-insurance, the insurers are only receiving a premium for a proportion of the entire value at risk, and any settlement will take into account using the formula:

$$\frac{\text{sum insured}}{\text{full value}} \times \text{loss}$$

For example, an insured suffers a fire loss of $50,000, due to an insured peril. His property is insured for $100,000. The insurers find that the actual value of the property is now $160,000. Average will be applied, using the formula above:

$$\frac{100,000}{160,000} \times 50,000 = \$31,250$$

When average operations reduce the amount payable, the insured really receives less than indemnity.[11] Because he is considered to be his own insurer for a portion of the risk and in a sense he should 「indemnity himself」 for the balance not received for the insurers.

1.3.3 Excess

Excess is amount of each and every claim that is not covered by the policy.[12] Excess are quite common on private car policies. In the event of accidental damage to the car itself, the insured might agree to pay the first $75, $100 or some other amount of the cost of repair. In theory, the insured himself becomes an insurer for the value of the excess. However, when the excess applies, the insured does receive less than the indemnity from the insurer.

1.3.4 Franchise

Franchise is a fixed amount to be paid by the insured himself in the event of a claim. However, once the amount of franchise is exceeded, the insurer pays the whole of the loss including the value of franchise.[13] Thus, if a policy has a franchise of $250, and a claim occurs for $250, the insured cannot receive anything from the insurer. However, if the claim is for $251, then he can receive the full amount, for the franchise limit has been exceeded.

1.3.5 Deductibles

A deductible is the name given to very large excess. An industrial insured may choose that it has the resources to meet fire claims up to $50,000 in any one period of insurance, and is confident in its own ability to prevent fires. It may approach an insurer and receive a discount from premium. In the event of a claim, it will settle for less than indemnity in order to obtain the savings in premium.

Section 2 Concept of subrogation

2.1 The meaning of subrogation

Subrogation means that after the insurer has indemnified the insured in the event of loss and damage, he is entitled to receive back from any other party liable.[14] Subrogation allows insurer to pursue any rights or remedies in the name of the insured.

2.2 Corollary of indemnity

When the contract is one of indemnity, subrogation can be applied.

Generally, if the insurer has indemnified the insured, any recovery will come from the third party. The insured cannot exercise his right until he is asked to do so by the insurer.

It should be noted that life contracts are not subject to the subrogation as they are not contracts of indemnity. If death was caused by negligence of another person, then the deceased's representatives are able to recover from that person in addition to the policy money. For example, if an airliner is crashed and causes the death of passengers, the beneficiaries can recover from the airliner company in addition to the policy money.

2.3 Extent of subrogation rights

Because of the connection between subrogation and indemnity, an insurer cannot recover more than he has paid out. In others words, the insurers must not make any profit by exercising their subrogation rights. There was such a case in 1962 in UK that the insurer has paid the insured £ 72,000, but due to the lapse of time between the claim payment and the recovery from the third party and due to the fact that the pound sterling has been devalued in the interval, the insured actually recovered £ 127,000 from the third party. It was held that the insurer was only entitled to £ 72,000[1].

2.4 The ways of arising subrogation

2.4.1 Rights arise out of tort

If the insured has sustained some damage, lost his right or incurred a liability due to the tortuous actions of some other person, then his insurer, having indemnified him for his loss, is entitled to take action to recover the outlay from the tortfeasor who is involved.

This arises in many ways. A motorist driving negligently may strike and damage a building. Trade persons may negligently leave factory doors open and thieves may steal some stock. A painter may drop ladders onto a machine so that it is damaged and production is lost. In each of these cases, the person suffering the loss could have had a policy to indemnify him. A household buildings policy, a theft

---

[1] Chris Parsons, David Green, Mike Mead. Contract Law and Insurance. Chartered Insurance Institute, 1995.

policy and an engineering external damage policy can cover all these risks.

2.4.2 Rights arise out of contract

The rights arising out of contract include tenancy agreements. Tenants agree to make good any damage to the property which they occupy. Prudent property owners would also maintain a policy of insurance. In the event of damage to the property, they may find it easier to recover under that policy. If they do recover from the insurer, they are not entitled to get the compensation from the tenant either.

2.4.3 Rights arise out of statute

In U. K, Public Order Act (1986) states that if a person suffers damage which is mentioned in the Act and is indemnified by the insurer, his insurers have the right in their own name to subrogate outlays from the police authority.[15]

Section 3 Concept of contribution

Contribution is derived from indemnity. It is also one of the important principles in insurance practice. This principle is often changed in practice by policy condition so that one insurer does not have to pay out for 100% of loss.

3.1 Meaning of contribution

Contribution is the right of an insurer to recover part of the amount paid from other insurers.[16] The fundamental point is that if an insurer has paid a full indemnity, he can recoup the payment of an equitable proportion from the other insurers. The principle of contribution enables the total claim to be shared between the different insurers.[17]

3.2 The condition in which contribution arises

Two or more policies of indemnity exist.
The policy covers a common interest.
The policy covers a common peril which gave rise to the loss.
The policy covers a common subject matter of insurance.

79

Each policy must be liable for the loss.

If there is an overlap between one policy and another, policies do not have to cover the same interests, or perils or subject matter of insurance.[18] A policy covering fire only would contribute with one covering fire, explosion and aircraft in respect of fire loss to the property insured.

3.3 The operation of contribution

Generally speaking, when an insured has more than one insurer, he can confine his claim to one of insurers. That insurer must meet the loss to the limit of his liability and can only call for contribution from the other after he has paid.[19] It is still very common in marine insurance.

In order to overcome this difficulty, most non-marine policies contain a contribution condition. The condition in most policies states that the insurer is liable only for his share and the insured is left to make a claim against the other insurer.[20] You should note that the condition does not require the insured to claim from the other policies.

3.4 Ways of contribution

The loss will be shared by insurers in their proportions. The purpose of the condition is really to prevent the insured claiming from one insurer only. For example, the sum insured of Company A is £ 1,000, the sum insured of Company B is £ 2,000 and the sum insured of Company C is £ 3,000, the loss is £ 1,500. According to the principle of contribution, we can know how much each company should pay. This approach is called independent liability method.

$$\text{Company A should pay} = 1,500 \times \frac{1,000}{1,000+2,000+3,000} = £\ 250$$

$$\text{Company B should pay} = 1,500 \times \frac{2,000}{1,000+2,000+3,000} = £\ 500$$

$$\text{Company C should pay} = 1,500 \times \frac{3,000}{1,000+2,000+3,000} = £\ 750$$

The exercising of an insurer's contribution rights or contribution rights must not interfere with or delay the insured's right to be indemnified within the terms of the policy.[21] For example, if an insured has given his name to an insurer for an action against a third party, the insurer cannot withhold the payment of the claim whether a recovery from the third party has been made or not.[22]

Professional terms

contract of indemnity	補償合同
exact financial compensation	確切的經濟補償
same financial position	同一經濟地位
enjoy benefit	享有利益
valid claim	有效索賠
cash payment	現金支付
electric payment	電子支付
authorized garage	授權的汽車修理廠
all in one roof	一切都在一個樓裡進行
enjoy discount	享有折扣
reinstatement	恢復原狀
measurement of indemnity	補償的計算
unvalued policy	不定值保險單
valued policy	定值保險單
subsequent market fluctuation	隨后的市價波動
amount of depreciation	折舊金額
cost of repairing damage	修理損失的費用
previous form	以往的形狀
allowance for depreciation	折舊費（率）
allowance for betterment	改良的費用
pecuniary insurance	現金損失保險，金錢損失保險
guarantee policy	保證保險單
dishonest of a cashier	收銀員的不誠實
business interruption insurance	企業中斷保險，利潤損失保險
out-of-court settlement	庭外解決
maximum amount recoverable	最高賠償金額
under-insurance	不足額保險
discount from premium	保險費折扣
corollary of indemnity	補償的必然結果
deceased's representatives	逝者的代表
airliner company	航空公司

policy money	保險補償金額
extent of subrogation right	代位追償的額度
make any profit	獲取利潤
exercising subrogation right	行使代位追償權
claim payment	索賠付款
arise out of tort	因……侵權引起
take action	採取行動
arise out of contract	因……合同引起
regardless of fault	無論有什麼缺點
tenancy agreement	租賃協議
prudent property owner	謹慎的財產所有者
arise out of statute	因……法定而引起
Public Order Act	《公共秩序法》
police authority	警察局
common interest	同一利益
common peril	同一風險
common subject matter of insurance	同一保險標的
call for contribution	需要分攤
non-marine policy	非水險
ways of contribution	分攤的方法
principle of contribution	分攤的原則
independent liability method	獨立責任方法
exercising insurer's contribution right	行使保險人的分攤權利
withhold payment of claim	截留索賠款

Notes to the chapter

1. Indemnity is one of the most important principles in insurance because the basic function of insurance is the financial compensation.

補償是保險的重要原則之一，因為保險的基本功能是經濟補償。

2. Indemnity can be defined as exact financial compensation. The indemnity should be sufficient to place the insured in the same financial position after a loss as he can enjoy the benefit before it occurs.

補償可以定義為確切的經濟賠償。損失發生以後，補償應該足以使被保險人恢復到相同的經濟狀況，就好像在損失發生以前他能享有這種利益一樣。

3. But if it is a personal accident policy which is bought by an employer on his staff, the

policy is intended to provide the employer with any amount he would have to pay to a sick employee for his wage.

但是如果是雇主為雇員購買的個人意外傷害保險，保險單旨在提供一筆錢給雇主，用以支付生病雇員的工資。

4. Insurance companies often authorize certain car garages to carry out repair work on damaged vehicles so that the cost of repair will be more reasonable and cheap.

保險公司經常授權某些汽車修理廠維修損壞的車輛，因而維修費用更合理、更便宜。

5. For example, the insured can drive or have his car pulled into the insurer's garage, complete a claim form, have the vehicle examined and have the work carried out all in one roof.

例如，被保險人將車開進修理廠或叫修理廠的人把車拖進來，填寫一張索賠單，安排人員檢查車輛等，所有工作在一個樓裡完成。

6. If there is a partial loss of goods, a settlement is made of a proportion of the agreed value according to the amount of depreciation.

如果是貨物的部分損失，賠償金額是扣除折舊金額後雙方達成協議的部分價值。

7. Then indemnity is the cost of that work less an allowance for depreciation as appropriate.

那麼補償金額就是施工的費用，減去適當的折舊費。

8. The indemnity sum for loss or damage to building can be calculated as the cost of repair or reconstruction at the time of loss, less an allowance for betterment.

計算建築物的損失補償金額等於損失發生時維修或重建的費用減去改良後的金額。

9. It is the amount of any award made by the court or it is an out-of-court settlement by the negotiation between the two parties

責任保險補償金額由法庭裁決或通過雙方協商庭外解決。

10. The maximum amount recoverable under any policy is limited by either the sum insured or the limit of indemnity.

保險單項下最大可能補償金額只限於保險金額或補償限額之內。

11. When average operations reduce the amount payable, the insured really receives less than indemnity.

當採取分攤方式減少了賠償金額時，被保險人實際上得到的賠償金額要少。

12. Excess is amount of each and every claim that is not covered by the policy.

免賠額是指每次索賠時，保險單不予承擔的金額。

13. Franchise is a fixed amount to be paid by the insured himself in the event of a claim. However, once the amount of franchise is exceeded, the insurer pays the whole of the loss including the value of franchise.

相對免賠額是在發生索賠時，由被保險人自己支付的一個固定金額。然而，一旦相對免賠額超出，保險人要支付全部賠償金額，包括相對免賠額。

14. Subrogation means that after the insurer has indemnified the insured in the event of loss and damage, he is entitled to receive back from any other party liable.

代位追償是指發生損失、保險人支付了被保險人的賠償後，保險人有權從負有責任的其他方追回賠款。

15. If a person suffers damage which is mentioned in the Act and is indemnified by the insurer, his insurers have the right in their own name to subrogate outlays from the police authority.

如果有人受到該法中提到的傷害，保險人就給予賠償，同時有權用保險人自己的名義向警察局提出追償。

16. Contribution is the right of an insurer to recover part of the amount paid from other insurers.

分攤是保險人的一種權利，是指一個保險人向被保險人支付賠款后，有權從另一位的保險人獲得賠款的一部分。

17. The principle of contribution enables the total claim to be shared between the different insurers.

分攤原則能夠使全部賠償金額在不同的保險人之間進行分攤。

18. If there is an overlap between one policy and another, policies do not have to cover the same interests, or perils or subject matter of insurance.

如果一張保險單與另一張保險單之間有重疊，那麼保險單之間不承保同一利益、或同一風險或保險標的。

19. That insurer must meet the loss to the limit of his liability and can only call for contribution from the other after he has paid.

保險人必須支付責任範圍內的損失，然后要求其他保險人分攤。

20. The condition in most policies states that the insurer is liable only for his share and the insured is left to make a claim against the other insurer.

大多數保險單的條款規定，保險人只承擔他的分攤金額，被保險人不得不向其他保險人索賠。

21. The exercising of an insurer's contribution rights or contribution rights must not interfere with or delay the insured's right to be indemnified within the terms of the policy.

行使保險人的代位追償或分攤權利不能妨礙或耽擱被保險人在保險單條款中得到賠償的權利。

22. The insurer cannot withhold the payment of the claim whether a recovery from the third party has been made or not.

無論保險人是否從第三方獲得賠償，保險人不能截留賠償款。

Exercises

I. Questions

1. Give definition of indemnity.
2. When a valid claim arises, how many methods are there for insurers adopting in providing indemnity?
3. Which method is often used as a method of providing indemnity in motor insurance?
4. Which method is often used as a method of providing indemnity in glass insurance?
5. Tell the difference between franchise and deductible.
6. Give the definition of subrogation.
7. What is contribution?
8. Do you think subrogation is derived from indemnity?

II. Find out a word in the text that means the same explanation and write down the word on the right column

1. An advantage or profit gained from something   1. _____
2. Money in coins or notes, as distinct from money orders, or credit   2. _____
3. A building for housing a motor vehicle or vehicles   3. _____
4. A deduction from the usual cost of something   4. _____
5. A regular gathering of people for the purchase and sale of provisions, livestock, and other commodities   5. _____
6. A reduction in the value of an asset over time, due to wear and tear 6. _____
7. An official agreement intended to resolve a dispute or conflict   7. _____
8. Acting with or showing care and thought for the future   8. _____
9. Power or right to give orders, make decisions, and enforce obedience 9. _____
10. Free from outside control, not subject to another's authority   10. _____

Ⅲ. True or false judgments

1. Indemnity can be defined as exact financial compensation, insufficient to place the insured in the same financial position after a loss as he can enjoy the benefit after it occurs.   (   )

2. In other words, life and personal accident policies are not contracts of indemnity, as the value of a person's life or limb cannot be measured by money.   (   )

3. Insurers make full use of repair as a method of providing indemnity in marine insurance.   (   )

4. In most cases, replacement refers to glass insurance. For example, broken windows and other items are replaced on behalf of insurers by glazing companies. Insurers can enjoy a discount from the glazing firms if insurers give vast amount of work for them.   (   )

5. In marine insurance, in the event of a partial loss of a ship, the indemnity is represented by the cost of repairing the damage.   (   )

6. In business interruption insurance, it is less difficult to establish indemnity. But with the help of the insured's accountants, it is necessary to try to establish what profit the firm would have made if the fire or other insured peril had not occurred.   (   )

7. Subrogation is one of the important concepts in insurance. Yet it is unnecessary for us to understand it thoroughly.   (   )

8. Franchise is a fixed amount to be paid by the insured in the event of a claim. However, once the amount of franchise is exceeded, the insurer pays the whole of the loss including the value of franchise.   (   )

9. Contribution is the right of an insurer who has paid a claim to the insured to recover part of the amount paid from other insurers if there are other policies covering the different loss.   (   )

10. The exercising of an insured's subrogation or contribution rights must not interfere with or delay the insured's right to be indemnified within the terms of the policy.   (   )

Ⅳ. Multiple choices

1. Insurance contract is contract of indemnity. _____ is derived from indemnity.

   A. Contribution   B. Contraction

   C. Consideration   D. Compensation

2. _____ can be defined as exact financial compensation, sufficient to place the insured in the same financial position after a loss as he can enjoy the benefit before it occurs.

   A. Contribution   B. Insurable interest

   C. Indemnity   D. Insurance

3. _____ policies are not contracts of indemnity, as the value of a person's life or limb cannot be measured by money.

A. Property   B. Marine   C. Life   D. Motor

4. When a valid claim arises, there are at least _____ methods that insurers can adopt in providing indemnity.

A. five   B. six   C. seven   D. four

5. In _____ insurance, cash payment is always made to the third party directly.

A. liability   B. property   C. Life   D. household

6. Insurers make full use of repair as a method of providing indemnity in _____ insurance.

A. motor   B. liability   C. medical   D. life

7. The principle of contribution enables the total claim to be shared between the different _____.

A. beneficiaries   B. applicants   C. insureds   D. insurers

8. In a valued policy, the insurable value is agreed by two parties in advance. _____ policy is valued insurance policy.

A. Motor   B. Cargo   C. Liability   D. Life

9. _____ is amount of each and every claim that is not covered by the policy.

A. Franchise   B. Excess   C. Deductible   D. Surpass

10. _____ is the right of an insurer who has paid a claim to the insured to recover part of the amount paid from other insurers if there are other policies covering the same loss.

A. Contribution   B. Compensation
C. Indemnity   D. Consideration

V. Translation from English to Chinese

1. The principle of indemnity relies heavily on financial evaluation, so we must consider the position of those policies where such valuation is difficult. In life and personal accident insurance, there is an unlimited interest, and in these cases indemnity is not possible. In other words, life and personal accident policies are not contracts of indemnity, as the value of a person's life or limb cannot be measured by money. But in the case of a personal accident policy bought by an employer on his staff, the policy is intended to provide him with any amount he would have to pay in wages to a sick employee.

2. Life contracts are not subject to the doctrine of subrogation as they are not contracts of indemnity. If death was caused by negligence of another person, then the deceased's representatives are able to recover from that person in addition to the policy money. So it follows that life contracts are not subject to subrogation as they are not contracts of indemnity. If death was caused by negligence of another person, then the deceased's representatives are able to recover from that person in addition to the policy money. For example, if an airliner is crashed and causes the death of passengers, the beneficiaries can recover from the airliner company in

addition to the policy money.

VI. Translation from Chinese to English
1. 補償原則依賴於財務評估。
2. 代位追償是從補償中派生出來的。
3. 保險人不能通過行使代位追償權而獲取利潤。
4. 除人壽保險合同之外，大多數財產保險合同是補償合同。
5. 人身保險不是補償合同，因為人的生命或肢體不能用金錢衡量。
6. 保險人可選擇賠付方式包括現金賠付、替換、修復和恢復原狀。
7. 在汽車保險中，保險人充分利用修復作為提供賠償的方法。
8. 在大多數情況下，替換指的是玻璃保險而言。

VII. Case analysis

An insured has written to the insurance company, saying that his TV set has been destroyed completely by fire. The claim is covered under her household policy and all the insurance company has to do is how much to pay. The TV set was 5 years old and cost $500 when it was purchased new. A similar TV set would cost $1,000 today. The insured agreed that the life of the TV set would have been 15 years and that her TV set had suffered normal wear and tear.

How much should insurance company pay under the indemnity policy? Write out the formula.

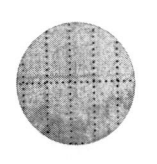

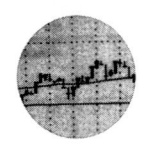

Chapter 6   **Insurance Contract**

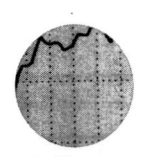

LEARNING OBJECTIVES:

☞ Understanding the meaning of general contract
☞ Learning about the essentials of contract
☞ Learning about the meaning of insurance contract
☞ Learning about the types of insurance contract

CONTENTS OF THIS CHAPTER:

☞ Section 1 Definition of general contract
☞ Section 2 Definition of insurance contract
☞ Section 3 The contents of insurance contract
☞ Section 4 The conclusion of insurance contract

Inquires

Excuse me, where is the underwriting department?

People make contracts for many purposes. For instance, there are contracts of insurance, contracts for the sale of goods and land, contracts of carriage, contracts of hire, contracts of employment and many others. In this chapter, we will discuss general contract and mainly the insurance contracts.

Section 1   Definition of general contract

A contract may be defined as a legally binding agreement.[1] In other words, a contract must be enforced or recognized by law. A valid contract including insurance contract needs five essentials.[2] They are agreement (offer and acceptance), the intention to create legal relation, the agreement in the form required by law and capacity. We will discuss them one by one in the following:

1.1 Agreement

Agreement is generally demonstrated by acceptance by one party of an offer made by another.[3] The person who makes an offer is called offeror and the person who accepts the offer is called offeree.[4]

An offer may be made in writing, orally or by conduct. It may be made to an individual, a group of people or the public. It is necessary for us to distinguish between true offer and statements.[5] Circulars, advertisements, prospectuses and the like are invitations to make an offer. Display of price-marked goods in a shop is only an invitation to make an offer, not a true offer.[6] Displays, advertisements and the like are offers in law. If an offer has been made, a contract will come into existence when the offer is accepted, provided that all the essential terms of the contract are agreed.

An insurance contract is concluded only after prolonged negotiations between proposer and insurer, often involving a broker or other intermediary.[7] In such cases, there may be a lengthy series of offers, rejections and counter-offers before a firm acceptance is made by one of the parties.

1.2 Intention to create legal relations

We have already defined a contract as a legally binding agreement. Even when two parties have reached an agreement, there may be no contract because they did not intend that their agreement should be legally binding. For example, in UK, a prostitute bought a carriage under an early form of hire-purchase contract. She failed to keep up the payments. She was sued by the render of the carriage. The court held that since the firm of coachbuilders knew that the carriage would be used to solicit customers, the contract was void and their action for arrears or debt failed.[8] It is held that contract in other immoral purposes is contrary to good morals. Besides, social and domestic agreements are not legally binding. No one supposes that accepting an invitation to a party or a wedding creates a contract.

1.3 Consideration

Consideration means some right and benefit made to one party, or some forbearance, detriment or loss suffered by the other.[9] In other words, when someone gets something, he will lose something at the same time. In insurance contract, for example, the insurer promises to provide indemnity for the risk, at the same time he will obtain insurance premiums for the risk.[10] And in a contract of sale, the seller may promise to supply goods. Meantime he will obtain the money of the goods. The law will not enforce a promise unless it is supported by consideration.[11] Consideration can also refer to the price that supports a promise.

1.4 Form required by law

In some cases the law requires a contract to be in a particular form. This will involve some type of written documentation because written documentation makes for greater certainty as to what has been agreed.[12] It may serve as a warning against entering into a contract too slightly.

1.5 Contractual capacity

Both parties who make a contract must have the capacity to perform the contract. The party of the contract must be a natural person[①] or corporate person who

---

① A natural person means that a man or a woman who has the capacity for action has reached the age required by law; he or she has a sound mind and can exercise his right and bear for the contract made by him or by her. A corporate person means that a man or a woman represents an enterprise, business and company to exercise his or her legal right and bear the legal liability for the contract made by him or by her.

can participate in the civil activity, exercise the civil right and bear the civil liability.

Section 2 Definition of insurance contract

2.1 The meaning of insurance contract

Insurance contract is a financial contract. It is defined in Article 10, Chapter II of Insurance Law of the People's Republic of China in 2009 as an insurance contract is an agreement in which a proposer and an insurer stipulate their respective obligations and rights in respect of an insurance policy. Insurance contract can be classified into the contract of property insurance and the contract of life assurance.

A property insurance contract refers to a contract, the subject matter of insurance of which a property and related interests associated therewith. A life assurance contract is a contract insuring a person's life and body.

2.2 The form of insurance contract

There are four kinds of form in insurance contracts. They are proposer form, temporary cover, insurance certificate and insurance policy.

2.2.1 Proposer form

Proposal form is also called application form. It is a written document which a proposer presents to the insurer when making an insurance contract.

2.2.2 Cover note

Cover note is also called temporary cover note. It is a proof existed before insurer issues a formal insurance policy. The legal validity of the temporary cover not is the same as the formal insurance policy.

2.2.3 Insurance certificate

Insurance certificate is a simplified insurance contract. Unlike insurance contract, insurance certificate does not list all the contents of a formal insurance contract. But it is of the same legal validity as an insurance contract. In China, in cargo insurance, in life insurance and in motor insurance, insurer frequently and largely issues insurance certificates.

2.2.4 Insurance policy

Insurance policy is formally drawn up and printed by insurer in advance. It is a formal written insurance contract made between the proposer and the insurer. It states the right and liability of the both parties. It is clearly that issuing of insurance policy means that the insurer has accepted the requirement offered by the insured.[13]

2.3 The subject, the object and content of the insurance contract

Insurance contract is a financial contract. Like any contract, it contains the subject, object and contents.

2.3.1 The subject of insurance contract

The subject of insurance contract can be classified into litigants who have direct relationship in the contract parties, such as proposer and insurer; persons who relate indirectly to insurance contract, such as beneficiary, insured; persons who act as intermediaries, such as insurance agent and insurance broker and assessor. (see the figure 6.1)

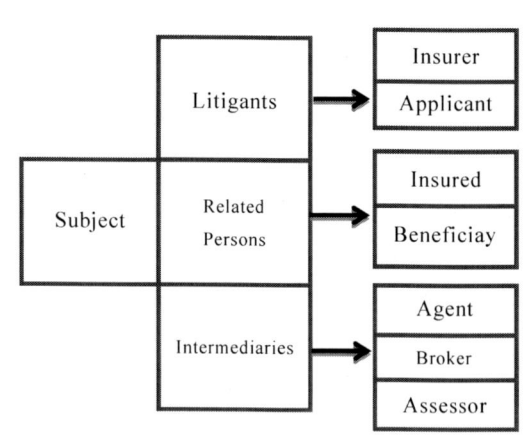

Subject	Litigants	Insurer
		Applicant
	Related Persons	Insured
		Beneficiay
	Intermediaries	Agent
		Broker
		Assessor

Figure 6.1

2.3.2 The object of insurance contract

The objects of insurance contract contain the subject matter of insurance and insurable interest. The subject matter of insurance can be any form of property, or an event that may result in the loss of a legal right or creation of a legal liability. Under a fire policy, the subject matter of insurance can be a building, stock or machinery. Under a liability policy, it can be a person's legal liability for injury or damage. As for life insurance, the subject matter of insurance is the life being insured. So far as the insurable interest is concerned, it is a basic requirement of any contract of insurance. Some scholars think that the object of an insurance contract is not the subject-matter of insurance itself but the insurable interest of the subject-matter of insurance.

Section 3 The contents of insurance contract

The contents of the insurance contract should be the subject matter of insurance with insurable interest to be covered by the insurer.[14] The main contents invariably drawn up beforehand by insurer in the form of provisions are available for the proposer to choose from. The main contents include:

3.1 Provisions

Insurance provisions contain basic conditions, additional clauses and warranty clauses. In any insurance contract, insurer draws up a standard insurance policy in advance in which there states the insurance liability, the extent of coverage, exclusions, the obligation of the insured, subrogation and arbitration, etc.

There are also optional clauses available for the insured to choose from, such as lease, mortgage clauses. Additional clauses refer to add up some clauses in addition to the basic clauses in order to meet the special need offered by proposer.[15] There are general additional clauses, such as leakage clause and risk of shortage. There are also particular additional clauses, such as risk on deck and risk of delivery.

As for warranty clauses are concerned, there are express terms and implied terms. Express terms are based on the words spoken by the parties or written down by them. The terms of motor policy may be contained partly in the policy and partly in the certificate of insurance issued in conjunction with it. Some of them may also lie in the proposal form completed by the insured. On the other hand, implied terms may be implied in fact, by custom or in law. For example, in marine insurance, the implied term is that the vessel must be seaworthy.

3.2　The main contents of the insurance policy

In addition to the provisions, according to Article 18 of Insurance Law of the People's Republic of China in 2009, an insurance contract shall contain the following:

Name and domicile of the insurer.

Names and domiciles of the proposer and the insured, as well as the name and domicile of the beneficiary in the case of personal insurance.

The subject matter of insurance.

Insurance liability and liability exemptions.

Term and starting date of coverage.

The insured amount.

Insurance premium and the payment method.

Method for payment of indemnities or insurance benefits.

Liability for breach of contract and dispute resolution.

Date of conclusion of contract.

Section 4　The conclusion of insurance contract

The conclusion of an insurance contract means a legal action of making an agreement between the insurer and insured on a fair and voluntary basis.[16] There are some principles in the conclusion of insurance contract.

4.1 The principle of entering an insurance contract

Article 11 of Insurance Law of the People's Republic of China in 2009 stipulates that conclusion of insurance contract should negotiate and follow the principle of fairness to determine the right and obligation between two parties. Any insurance contract should be concluded voluntarily, except for those insurance made compulsory by laws and administrative regulations.[17]

4.1.1 Fair and mutual

It means that when entering into an insurance contract, it must make both parties benefit from it. Both parties can enjoy their rights as well as bear their obligations and liability equally in the contract.

4.1.2 Consulting and discussing

It refers to the fact that when entering into an insurance contract, both parties should stand in the complete legal position, consulting and discussing the contract. Any party cannot force his will upon another party when entering into a contract.

4.1.3 Voluntary

It means that when entering into an insurance contract, any party is independent. He is entitled to enter into a contract within the law and the way without being threatened, forced and fraudulent.

4.2 The novation of an insurance contract

When an insurance contract is concluded, generally speaking, it will be carried out till it is terminated. However, sometimes one party wants to modify some particulars of the contract because some different changes occur. Since insurance contacts are long term ones, it is very common for one of the parties to modify the contract.

4.2.1 Novation of the subject of insurance contract

It refers to the modification of the insurer, the applicant, the insured and the beneficiary. When the insurer is bankrupted or dissolved, the contract must be transferred to another insurer. In property insurance, if the insured property is sold or transferred or inherited, the applicant or the insured has to be modified. In life insurance, the insured person's life is the subject-matter of insurance. Therefore the modification of the insured is the change of the subject of insurance contract.[18] In practice, the modification of the insured leads to the cancel of the contract. In fact, the change of life contract has something to do with the modification of the applicant or the beneficiary.[19]

4.2.2 Novation of content of insurance contract

The novation of object of insurance contract refers to the change of increasing or reducing the value of the subject matter of insurance.[20] It also refers to the change of insurance liability, insurance premium and insured amounts and so on. When the insured wants to modify the sum insured, first he should make an offer to the insurer. After the insurer accepted the offer, the insurer issues an endorsement.

4.3 Transfer of rights of insurance contracts

The subject-matter of an insurance contract will often be transferred from one person to another. For example, a motor policyholder may sell his car to another. The insured under a household buildings policy may sell his house. Assignment of the subject-matter does not carry with it any assignment of the policy.[21] If the insured disposes of the subject-matter of the insurance, the usual effect will bring the contact to an end.

The right to recover money under an insurance contract can be transferred to another person. Here the entire contract is not assigned, but only the benefit of it. There is no change in the subject-matter of the insurance contract. The insured can assign the benefit of his household policy to a builder as a means of paying for the repair of storm damage which the policy covers.

The assignment of an entire insurance contract is subject to some limiting factors. In motor insurance, the terms of cover and premium will depend not only on the vehicle to be insured but also the age, occupation, experience and driving record of the insured. The insurance contract cannot be assigned without the consent of the insurer in property insurance. If Jack sells his car or his house to Rose, Rose's insurer will ask her to submit a new contract. Because of the limitations, few insurance contracts are freely assignable except marine cargo policies. The ownership of cargo may change several times in the course of a voyage, but the risk does not change as a result of a change in the ownership of the goods.[22]

Professional terms

general contract	一般合同
essential of contract	合同要素
types of insurance contract	保險合同種類
legally binding agreement	法律約束的協議
valid contract	有效合同
make an offer	提出要約
accept the offer	接受要約
a group of people	一群人
invitations to make an offer	提出要約的邀請
price-marked goods	明碼標價的商品
counter-offers	還價，反要約
a lengthy series of offers	漫長的要約
early form of hire-purchase contract	早期租賃合同
immoral purpose	不道德的目的
contrary to good moral	與良好道德相違背

domestic agreement	家庭協議
written documentation	書面文件
natural person	自然人
corporate person	法人
civil activity	民事活動
civil right	民事權力
civil liability	民事責任
contractual capacity	履行合同能力
financial contract	經濟合同
proposer form	投保單
temporary cover	臨時保單
insurance certificate	保險憑證
insurance policy	保險單
formal written insurance contract	正式的書面保險合同
issuing of insurance policy	保險單簽發
subject of insurance contract	保險合同主體
objects of insurance contract	保險合同客體
creation of a legal liability	法律責任的建立
insurable interest of the subject-matter of insurance	保險標的的保險利益
content of the insurance contract	保險合同的內容
basic condition	基本條件
additional clause	附加條款
warranty clause	保證條款
standard insurance policy	標準保險單
in advance	提前
extent of coverage	承保範圍
subrogation and arbitration	代位追償與仲裁
optional clause	選擇性條款
general additional clause	一般附加條款
particular additional clause	特別附加條款
warranty clause	擔保條款
mortgage clause	抵押條款
express term	明示條款
implied terms	默示條款
legal action	法律責任
administrative regulation	行政法規

bear obligation　　　　承擔責任
enter into insurance contract　　簽訂保險合同
motor policyholder　　　汽車保單持有人
household buildings policy　　房屋建築保險單
assignment of the subject-matter　　保險標的的轉讓
assignment of the policy　　保單的轉讓
insurance certificate　　　保險憑證
insurance agent　　　保險代理人
insurance broker　　　保險經紀人
insurance assessor　　　保險公估人

Notes to the chapter

1. A contract may be defined as a legally binding agreement.

合同可以定義為具有法律約束力的一種協議。

2. A valid contract including insurance contract needs five essentials.

有效合同包括保險合同需要五個方面的要素。

3. Agreement is generally demonstrated by acceptance by one party of an offer made by another.

協議通常是由一方提出要約，另一方加以承諾進行的。

4. The person who makes an offer is called offeror and the person who accepts the offer is called offeree.

提出要約的人稱之為「offeror」，接受要約的人稱之為「offeree」。

5. It is necessary for us to distinguish between true offer and statements.

我們有必要區分真正的要約與聲明。

6. Circulars, advertisements, prospectuses and the like are invitations to make an offer.

傳單、廣告、說明書以及諸如此類的東西都是引起要約的邀請。

7. An insurance contract is concluded only after prolonged negotiations between proposer and insurer, often involving a broker or other intermediary.

保險合同的簽訂要經過投保人和保險人長時間協商，經常有經紀人和其他中間人參與。

8. The court held that since the firm of coachbuilders knew that the carriage would be used to solicit customers, the contract was void and their action for arrears or debt failed.

法庭認為既然馬車公司知道馬車用來拉客，那麼這個合同是無效的。他們起訴拖欠的款或債務失敗。

9. Consideration means some right and benefit made to one party, or some forbearance,

101

detriment or loss suffered by the other.

對價指的是一方獲得的權利和所得到的利益，另一方承受的忍耐、傷害和損失。

10. In insurance contract, for example, the insurer promises to provide indemnity for the risk, at the same time he will obtain insurance premiums for the risk.

例如，保險合同中保險人許諾提供風險的補償，同時他將獲得承擔風險的保險費。

11. The law will not enforce a promise unless it is supported by consideration.

法律將不會強制執行一個許諾，除非該許諾有對價的支撐。

12. This will involve some type of written documentation because written documentation makes for greater certainty as to what has been agreed.

這將涉及一些書面的公文，因為書面的公文對於達成的協議更具確定性。

13. It is clearly that issuing of insurance policy means that the insurer has accepted the requirement offered by the insured.

顯而易見，保險單的簽發意味著保險人已經接受了被保險人提出的要求。

14. The contents of the insurance contract should be the subject matter of insurance with insurable interest to be covered by the insurer.

保險合同的內容就是由保險人承保的具有保險利益的保險標的。

15. Additional clauses refer to add up some clauses in addition to the basic clauses in order to meet the special need offered by proposer.

附加條款指的是在基本條款后增加一些條款，以便滿足投保人提出的特殊需要。

16. The conclusion of an insurance contract means a legal action of making an agreement between the insurer and insured on a fair and voluntary basis.

簽訂保險合同是指保險人和被保險人按照自願的原則達成協議的法律行為。

17. Article 11 of Insurance Law of the People's Republic of China in 2009 stipulates that conclusion of insurance contract should negotiate and follow the principle of fairness to determine the right and obligation between two parties. Any insurance contract should be concluded voluntarily, except for those insurance made compulsory by laws and administrative regulations.

《中華人民共和國保險法》第十一條規定，訂立保險合同，應當協商一致，遵循公平原則確定各方的權利和義務。除法律、行政法規規定必須保險的外，保險合同自願訂立。

18. Therefore the modification of the insured is the change of the subject of insurance contract.

因此，被保險人的變更就是保險合同主體的變更。

19. In fact, the change of life contract has something to do with the modification of the applicant or the beneficiary.

事實上，人壽保險合同的變更與投保人或受益人變更有關。

20. The novation of object of insurance contract refers to the change of increasing or reducing the value of the subject matter of insurance.

保險合同客體的變更指的是保險標的價值的增加與減少。

21. Assignment of the subject-matter does not carry with it any assignment of the policy.

保險標的的轉移不會因保險單的轉移而轉移。

22. The ownership of cargo may change several times in the course of a voyage, but the risk does not change as a result of a change in the ownership of the goods.

雖然貨物的所有權在航行中轉變數次，但是風險並未隨貨物所有權的改變而改變。

Exercises

Ⅰ. Questions

1. What is a general contract?
2. Tell the essentials of a valid contract.
3. Give the definition of insurance contract.
4. Give the definition of consideration.
5. Explain the natural person.
6. What are express terms and implied terms?
7. What is the subject of insurance?
8. Consideration is very important in the contract. Give some examples to explain it.

Ⅱ. Match up the explanations of the left column with the word on the right column

1. A written or verbal request inviting someone to go somewhere or to do something
2. The amount of money expected, required, or given in payment for something
3. Material that provides official information or evidence or that serves as a record
4. Lasting for only a limited period of time; not permanent
5. A thing which has been made or invented
6. A legal agreement by which a bank, lends money at interest in exchange for taking title of the debtor's property
7. The condition of being morally or legally bound to do something

1. agent (　　)
2. certificate (　　)
3. invitation (　　)
4. broker (　　)
5. price (　　)
6. creation (　　)
7. mortgage (　　)

8. A document confirming that someone has reached a certain level of achievement in a course of study or training   8. documentation ( )

9. A person who acts on behalf of another, in particular   9. obligation ( )

10. A person who buys and sells goods or assets for others   10. temporary ( )

III. True or false judgments

1. A valid contract including insurance contract needs four essentials. ( )

2. Display of price-marked goods in a shop is a true offer. ( )

3. The contract was void and their action for arrears or debt failed. It is held that contract in other immoral purposes is contrary to good morals. ( )

4. Social and domestic agreements are not legally binding. No one supposes that accepting an invitation to a party or a wedding creates a contract. ( )

5. Consideration means some right, profit or benefit made to one party, or some forbearance, detriment or loss suffered by the other. ( )

6. In some cases the law requires a contract to be in a particular form. This will involve some type of written documentation because written documentation makes for less certainty as to what has been agreed. ( )

7. Proposal form is also called application form. It is a written document which a proposer presents to brokers when making an insurance contract. ( )

8. Insurance certificate also lists all the contents of a formal insurance contract. In China, in cargo insurance, in life insurance and in motor insurance, insurer seldom issues insurance certificates. ( )

9. In any insurance contract, insurer draws up a standard insurance policy in advance in which there states the insurance liability, the extent of coverage, exclusions, the obligation of the insured, subrogation and arbitration, etc. ( )

10. Because of the limitations, few insurance contracts are freely assignable except marine cargo policies. ( )

IV. Multiple choices

1. _____ is generally demonstrated by acceptance by one party of an offer made by another.

     A. Contract   B. Agreement   C. Decision   D. Contest

2. The person who makes an offer is called offeror and the person who accepts the offer is called _____.

     A. insured   B. applicant   C. offeree   D. insurer

3. A _____ person means that a man or a woman who has the capacity for action has reached the age required by law, has a sound mind and can exercise his right and bear liability.

  A. natural   B. corporate   C. female   D. male

4. Secondly, the right to recover money under an _____ can be transferred to another person.

  A. agreement   B. insurance contract   C. offer   D. acceptance

5. A _____ insurance contract is a contract insuring a person's life and body. The applicant has insurable interests over himself or herself, the applicant's spouse, children and parents.

  A. property   B. motor   C. medical   D. life

6. Proposal form is a written document which a proposer presents to _____ when he makes an insurance contract with the insurer.

  A. insurer   B. broker   C. agent   D. seller

7. Unlike insurance contract, _____ does not list all the contents of a formal insurance contract. But it is of the same legal validity as an insurance contract.

  A. insurance policy   B. cover note

  C. insurance certificate   D. proposal form

8. _____ is formally drawn up and printed by insurer. It states the right and liability of the both parties.

  A. insurance policy   B. insurance certificate

  C. cover note   D. proposal form

9. In _____ insurance, the terms of cover and premium will depend not only on the vehicle to be insured but also on the age, occupation, experience and driving record of the insured.

  A. property   B. motor   C. life   D. marine

10. Because of the limitations, few insurance contracts are freely assignable except _____ policies.

  A. marine cargo   B. property   C. motor   D. life

V. Translation from English to Chinese

1. Consideration means some right, profit or benefit made to one party, or some forbearance, detriment or loss suffered by the other. In insurance contract, for example, the insurer promises to provide cover against certain risks; and in a contract of sale, the seller may promise to supply certain goods. The law will not enforce a promise unless it is supported by consideration. Consideration can be described as the price that supports a promise.

2. For example, in UK, a prostitute bought a carriage under an early form of hire-pur-

chase contract. She failed to keep up the payments. She was sued by the render of the carriage. The court held that since the firm of coachbuilders knew that the carriage would be used to solicit customers, the contract was void and their action for arrears or debt failed. It is held that contract in other immoral purposes is contrary to good morals.

VI. Translation from Chinese to English

1. 社交協議和家庭協議沒有法律約束力。接受一方的邀請或參加一個人的婚禮不會產生建立一個合同關係。

2. 法律不會對許諾強制執行，除非許諾有對價的支撐。

3. 簽署合同的雙方必須具備履行合同的能力。

4. 保險憑證是保險合同的簡化形式。保險單是由保險人起草和印刷出來的。

5. 保險合同的訂立是指保險人與被保險人在公平自願的基礎上達成協議的一種法律行為。

6. 財產保險中，如果被保險的財產被出售、被轉移或被繼承，投保人或被保險人必須更改。

7. 在汽車保險中，承保條款和保費不僅依據被保險的車輛，而且依據被保險人的年齡、職業、經驗以及被保險人的駕駛紀錄。

8. 由於有這些限制，除了海上貨物保險單以外，保險合同不能自由轉讓。

VII. Case analysis

A son takes the family business over from his father, who wishes to retire from active business life. Several years later, the son wishes to expand the business, which is that of a self-employed haulage contractor, by purchasing another vehicle. The cost of this will be $20,000 and he requests a loan of $15,000 from his father to enable him to purchase the vehicle. The father agrees to provide the son with the loan subject to two conditions:

1. The son takes a life insurance policy out on his own life for $15,000 making the father beneficiary.

2. The son takes out a policy in the joint names of father and son to cover the vehicle, so that in the event of vehicle being damaged or destroyed, the father's interest is also taken care of.

Do you think the life underwriters will agree to the arrangement?

Do you think the motor insurers will agree to the arrangement?

What recommendations can you make in respect of the proposed arrangements?

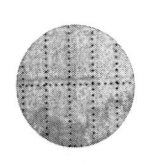

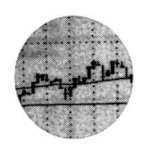

Chapter 7   Insurance Market

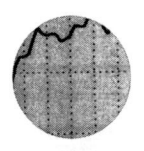

LEARNING OBJECTIVES：

☞Learning about London insurance market
☞Understanding the meaning of insurance market
☞Learning about the Lloyd's market
☞Learning about insurance intermediaries

CONTENTS OF THIS CHAPTER：

☞Section 1 Concept of London insurance market
☞Section 2 London insurance companies
☞Section 3 London insurance organizations
☞Section 4 Lloyd's Market
☞Section 5 Insurance intermediaries

At first we should know what a market is. A market is place where a group of people, individuals and members of organizations, come and go for the purpose of trade transaction. They are the actual or potential buyers or sellers of a product. As for insurance market, however, there is no single place in the country or in a town where the buyers, sellers and middlemen meet to transact insurance.[1]

Section 1　Concept of London insurance market

1.1　Definition of London insurance market

There is no strict definition of the term 「London Insurance Market」. Some specialists believe that the core of its activity is the conduct of 「internationally traded insurance and reinsurance business」.[2] The business traded is almost exclusively non-life insurance and reinsurance.

1.2　Features of London insurance market

London insurance market is a 「subscription market」 in which insurances and reinsurances are placed by insurance brokers with two or more insurers or reinsurers who subscribe to a 「slip」 prepared by the broker.[3] The slip contains details of the risk to be insured or reinsured. The leading underwriter indicates the terms for acceptance of the business and each insurer states the share of the risk it is willing to accept on the slip.[4]

Among international markets, London is unique market that is concentrated highly in terms of geographical location. It comprises a large number of insurers and intermediaries located in the City of London and its close vicinity.[5] They are active in placing and accepting direct insurance and reinsurance business, which enables brokers to know personally the strengths, expertise and reputations of the underwriters and the insurers, and to gain access readily to the total market's underwriting capacity.[6] Buyers can also meet with their insurers, and market information is rapidly disseminated among all participants.

London's main attractions to foreign insurers and reinsurers to write international business are the mode of operation and reputation for innovation and security.[7] These are the main features. The larger is the market, the greater is its attraction to brokers, buyers and potential new clients. Many firms supply ancillary services, such as actuarial, accounting, banking, other financial, legal, loss adjusting and so on.

Section 2　London insurance companies

2.1　The Department of Trade and Industry

The Department of Trade and Industry (DTI) was a United Kingdom government department formed on 19 October 1970. It was replaced with the creation of the Department for Business, Enterprise and Regulatory Reform and the Department for Innovation, Universities and Skills on 28 June 2007.

In 1983, the Departments of Trade and Industry were reunited. The Department of Energy was re-merged back into the DTI in 1992, but various media-related functions transferred to the Department for National Heritage. Until it was succeeded in June 2007 the DTI continued to set the energy policy of the United Kingdom.[8]

After the 2005 general election, the DTI was renamed to the Department for Productivity, Energy and Industry, but the name reverted to Department of Trade and Industry less than a week later.[9]

A company wishing to transact insurance business in the UK must be licensed by the Department of Trade and Industry under the provisions of the Insurance Companies Act 1982.[10]

The insurance and reinsurance companies operating in the London Market fall into five groups: the companies that are members of the IUA; the P & I clubs; the fringe companies and the contact offices. According to a report in 2013, there are 105 insurance and reinsurance companies in UK in London market.

Besides the P & I clubs, the combined membership of the IUA and LIRMA provides a good guide to the number of London Market companies. In addition to this, there are a very small number of fringe companies.

Traditionally, companies operating in the market have located their underwriting rooms within a short walking distance of Lloyd's building. The advantages for brokers of this geographical concentration of the market have been reinforced by recent developments within the company's market.[11]

2.2　Major insurance companies

2.2.1　Aviva (plc.)

Aviva (plc.) is a British multinational insurance company headquartered in London. It has around 31 million customers across 16 countries. In the UK Aviva is the largest general insurer and a leading life and pensions provider. In addition, Aviva has a focus on five markets in Europe and in Asia; the company is focused on the growth markets of China and South East Asia. Aviva is also the second largest general insurer in Canada. Its net income is £ 2.151 billion in 2013.

The name of the company upon its formation in May 2000 was CGNU (Commercial Union, General Accident and Norwich Union). In April 2002 the company's shareholders voted to change the company name to Aviva plc., an invented word derived from viva, the Latin for life and designed to be short, memorable and work worldwide. In April 2008 Aviva announced that it would adopt the Aviva name as its worldwide consumer-facing brand, and that the Norwich Union brand would be phased out in the United Kingdom.

Aviva has a primary listing on the London Stock Exchange and is a constituent of the FTSE 100 Index.[12]

2.2.2　RSA Insurance Group (plc.)

RSA Insurance Group (plc.) is the second-largest general insurer in the United Kingdom. It is the merger between Royal and Sun Alliance in 1996 and changed to the name RSA Insurance Group on 20th, May 2008. Sun Alliance was itself a product of the merger in 1959 of The Sun founded in 1710, with The Alliance founded in 1824. Royal Insurance was founded in 1845. It acquired Liverpool & London and Globe Insurance Company in 1919.

RSA Insurance Group is a multinational general insurance company headquartered in London. RSA operates in 32 countries and provides insurance products and services in more than 140 through a global network of local partners.[13] Its revenue is £ 9,258 million and operating income is £ 371 million and net income is £ 338 million in 2013.

RSA is listed on the London Stock Exchange and is a constituent of the FTSE

100 Index.

2.2.3　Legal & General Group (plc.)

Legal & General Group (plc.) is a British multinational financial services company headquartered in London. Its products include life insurance, general insurance, pensions and investments. It has operations in the United Kingdom, Egypt, France, Germany, the Gulf, India, the Netherlands and the United States. As at 6 August 2013 it had total funds under management of £ 433 billion.

Legal & General is listed on the London Stock Exchange and is a constituent of the FTSE 100 Index.

2.2.4　Prudential (plc.)

Prudential (plc.) is a British multinational life insurance and financial services company headquartered in London. It was founded in London in May 1848 as The Prudential Mutual Assurance Investment and Loan Association to provide loans to professional and working people.

Prudential's largest division is Prudential Corporation Asia, which has over 13 million customers across 12 Asian markets and is a top-three provider of life insurance in Hong Kong, India, Indonesia, Malaysia, Singapore, the Philippines and Vietnam.[14] Its Prudential UK division has around 7 million customers and is a leading provider of life insurance and pensions in the UK. Prudential also owns Jackson National Life Insurance Company, which is one of the largest life insurance providers in the United States, and M&G Investments, a Europe-focused asset manager with total assets under management of £ 228 billion at 31 December 2012.

Prudential has a primary listing on the London Stock Exchange and is also a constituent of the FTSE 100 Index.

Section 3　London insurance organizations

3.1　Association of British Insurers

Association of British Insurers (ABI) is the main trade association of insurance companies in the UK. According to the Association, it has around 300 companies in membership. Between them, they provide 90% of domestic insurance services sold in the UK. ABI member companies account for almost 20 per cent of investments in London's stock market.[15] Its members are major tax contributors, paying £ 10.4 billion in the 2010 / 2011 tax year. The organization is funded by members' subscriptions.

Formed in 1985 by the merger of a number of specialist insurance company associations, including the British Insurance Association, the Life Offices' Association, the Fire Offices Committee, the Accident Offices Association, the Industrial Life Offices Association and the Accident Offices Association (Overseas), the UK insurance industry is the largest in Europe and the third largest in the world.[16]

The main objectives of ABI include the promotion of the interests of its members, and the representation of their views to the government and other agencies.[17] It prepares a number of statistical and other publications, including an annual report, and consumer advice and crime prevention leaflets.[18]

Its offices are at 51-55 Gresham Street in the City of London, just west of the Guildhall, London. St. Paul's tube station is to the south-west. The ABI employs around 100 people. The association is a member of Insurance Europe.

The ABI represents the collective interests of the UK's insurance industry. The Association speaks out on issues of common interest, helps to inform and participate in debates on public policy issues, and also acts as an advocate for high standards of customer service in the insurance industry.

3.2 International Underwriting Association (IUA)

The International Underwriting Association of London, better known as the IUA, represents companies that trade in the London insurance market outside Lloyd's. They include branches or subsidiaries of nearly all the world's largest international insurance and reinsurance companies. The exact size of IUA members' contribution to the London market is not known. They wrote a total of at least £ 10 billion premiums during 2009, a figure that does not include income processed outside the London market bureau. This business is wholesale, the bulk being made up of insurance for large multinational companies or reinsurance.[19] Most of it is international, brought into London by brokers. The IUA provides a forum for discussing market issues and providing technical support to practitioners.[20]

The IUA was formed in January 1998 from the merger of the London International Insurance and Reinsurance Market Association (LIRMA) and the Institute of London Underwriters (ILU). The main reason for the merger was the desire to give the company market in London a single voice in dealings with government, regulators and other insurance bodies.[21] Since the ILU had been formed in 1884, the IUA can claim to go back more than a century. The association has always made reform of the London market a top priority, especially the replacement of out-of-date processes and increased use of technology to conduct business.[22] This led in 1999 to the creation of the IUA-Lloyd's Forum. This soon expanded to include brokers and eventually evolved into the London Market Group, which is still active today.

3.3 Fringe companies

The term 「fringe companies」in the past referred to companies that operated on the fringes of the Lloyd's market.[23] Today, although the term is less frequently encountered, there are companies authorized under the Insurance Companies Act to transact insurance business in Britain, which may write direct insurance and reinsurance business on the London market. Normally they are relatively small companies which will take a small line on risks led by a Lloyd's syndicate.[24] At the time of writing, there are very few companies in that category, but their number does tend to vary with the state of the underwriting cycle, with companies entering the market at times when capacity is scare, and leaving when premium rate are falling and losses rising.

3.4 Contact offices

Besides companies authorized to write insurance business in Britain, some foreign companies maintain an offer in London to keep in contact with the market, and to transmit to their head offices for acceptance any business which may be offered to them by brokers.[25] It is an offence for such a company to actually underwrite the business in Britain.

3.5 Protection and indemnity insurance

Protection and indemnity insurance, more commonly known as P&I

insurance, is a form of international maritime insurance provided by a P&I Club, a mutual insurance association that provides risk pooling, information and representation for its members, typically ship-owners and ship-operators.[26] Unlike other marine insurance company, which reports to its shareholders, a P&I club only reports to its members.

P&I clubs provide insurance for broader, indeterminate risks that marine insurers usually do not cover, such as third party risks.[27] These risks include a carrier's liability to a cargo-owner for damage to cargo, a ship-owner's liability after a collision, environmental pollution and P&I war risk insurance, or legal liability due to acts of war affecting the ship.

The European Union Directive was implemented in all 27 member States by January 1, 2012.[28] The Directive requires compulsory P&I to cover for EU ships and for foreign ships in EU waters and ports. Foreign vessels that do not comply with the Directive will be expelled and refused entry into any EU port, although ships may be allowed some time to comply before expulsion.[29]

Section 4　Lloyd's Market

4.1　History of Lloyd's

Ever since the emergence of Britain as a maritime power and London as its largest trading port, Lloyd's of London has played the central role of a marine insurance market.[30]

Lloyd's of London was founded by Edward Lloyd at his coffee house on Tower Street in the 17th century. The coffee house was a popular place for sailors, merchants, and ship owners and Lloyd provided them with reliable shipping news. The shipping industry community came to the place to discuss deals among themselves, including insurance. Just after Christmas 1691, the house was moved to Lombard Street. After Lloyd's death in 1713, the participating members of the insurance arrangement formed a committee and moved to the Royal Exchange on Cornhill as The Society of Lloyd's.

4.2 Structure of Lloyd's

Lloyd's is not an insurance company, it is an insurance market of members. As the oldest continuously active insurance marketplace in the world, Lloyd's has retained some unusual structures and practices that differ from all other insurance providers today. Originally created as a non-incorporated association of subscribing members, it was incorporated by the Lloyd's Act 1871 and is currently governed under the Lloyd's Acts of 1871 through to 1982.

Lloyd's itself does not underwrite insurance business, leaving that to its members. Instead, the Society operates effectively as a market regulator, setting rules under which members operate and offering centralized administrative services to those members.

4.3　Businesses at Lloyd's

There are two classes of people and firms active at Lloyd's. The first are Members or providers of capital. The second are agents, brokers and other professionals who support the Members, underwrite the risks.

The capital which requires supporting the underwriting of insurances and reinsurances is supplied by investors, known as 「Names」, who conduct their business through syndicates run by managing agents on the Names' behalf.[31] The insurance business underwritten at Lloyd's is predominantly general insurance and reinsurance, although in 2013 there were five syndicates writing term life assurance.

In 2011, over £ 23.44 billion of gross premiums were transacted in the Lloyd's market and in the aggregate it made a pre-tax loss of £ 516 million, driven by a number of significant natural disasters which gave rise to the highest ever annual level of claims for Lloyd's.[32] In 2012, Lloyd's made a pre-tax profit of £ 2.77 billion on a record £ 25.50 billion of gross written premiums.

Section 5　Insurance intermediaries

5.1　Insurance Brokers

Article 118 of Insurance Law of the People's Republic of China states that an insurance broker is an institution, based upon the interests of the proposer, provides intermediary services for the conclusion of an insurance contract between the proposer and insurer, and that charges a commission fee in accordance with the law.

We can also say that an insurance broker is an individual or firm whose full-time occupation is the placing of insurance with insurance companies. The insured can obtain independent advice on a wide range of insurance matters from a broker, without direct cost to himself. For example, the broker will advise on insurance needs, best type of cover and its restrictions, best market, claims procedure, obligations placed on the insured by policy conditions.

From the insurer's point of view, negotiations with brokers are easier and speedier because only intricate points or special requirements require detailed discussion. It will save time and money on routine matters.

The vast majority of commercial insurance will be transacted through a registered broker. In larger cases, these brokers will provide an in invaluable service to large corporations. Besides, the broker may also handle certain claims, draft policy wordings, carry out risk surveys, and provide risk management service and so on.

Brokers play a key role in bringing business to the insurance market (see Table 7.1). The insurance broker will choose a leading underwriter, who decides on the rate to be charged and conditions of the insurance and will assume the largest percentage of the risk. With the terms and conditions in place the slip will be taken to other insurers until 100% of the risk is placed after securing agreement from the insured.

An insurance broker shall be liable for damages or losses caused to the applicant or the insured due to the negligence of the insurance broker in the course of transacting insurance business. The commission of the insurance brokers comes from the insurance companies.

Table 7.1   The World's 10 Largest Insurance Brokers in 2013

Rank	Company	Country	Brokerage revenue in 2013	Staff	Website
1	Marsh & McLennan Cos. Inc.	USA	$12,270,000,000	55,000	www.mmc.com
2	Aon P.L.C.	UK	$11,787,000,000	66,000	www.aon.com
3	Willis Group Holdings P.L.C.	UK	$3,633,000,000	18,000	www.willis.com
4	Arthur J. Gallagher & Co.	USA	$2,742,000,000	16,336	www.ajg.com
5	Jardine Lloyd Thompson Group P.L.C.	UK	$1,746,454,140	5,165	www.jltgroup.com
6	BB & T Insurance Holdings Inc.	USA	$1,582,443,400	6,406	www.insurance.ttb.com
7	Brown & Brown Inc.	USA	$1,355,502,535	6,992	www.bbinsurance.com
8	Wells Fargo Insurance Services USA Inc.	USA	$1,350,022,000	5,689	www.wellsfargo.com
9	Hub International Ltd.	USA	$1,147,560,000	6,389	www.hubinternatioal.com
10	Lockton Cos. L.L.C.	USA	$1,116,822,000	5,300	www.lockton.com

Since the promulgation of Insurance Law of People's Republic of China in 1995 and the establishment of China Insurance Regulatory Commission in 1998, the insurance market in China has become more and more mature. Under this situation, the broker's industry developed fast. Since the ratification of the establishment of Changcheng Insurance Brokers Company, Ltd. Jiang Tai Insurance Brokers Company, Ltd and Shanghai Dongda Insurance Brokers Company, Ltd. (see Table 7.2), there have been 434 insurance brokers companies.

Table 7.2　　　　China's 10 Largest Insurance Brokers in 2013①

Rank	Company	Head office	Website
1	Yingda Chang'An Insurance Brokers Group Ltd.	Xi'an	http://www.caib.sgcc.com.cn/
2	Aon-COFCO Insurance Brokers Co., Ltd.	Shanghai	http://www.aon-cofco.com.cn/
3	Union Insurance Broker CO.,Ltd.	Beijing	http://www.chinauib.com/
4	Jiang Tai Insurance Brokers Co., Ltd.	Beijing	http://www.jiangtai.com/
5	Marsh (Beijing) Insurance Brokers Co,. Ltd.	Beijing	http://asia.marsh.com/china
6	Willis Insurance Brokers Co., Ltd.	Shanghai	http://www.willis.cn/
7	Jing Sheng Insurance Brokers Co., Ltd.	Beijing	http://www.jingsheng.cn
8	Air Union Insurance Brokers Co,.Ltd.	Beijing	http://www.air-union.com/forview/homecell/home_cn.jsp
9	Changcheng Insurance Brokers Co,. Ltd.	Guangzhou	http://www.ccib.com.cn/chn/home/Index.asp
10	Hua Tai Insurance Agency & Consultant Service Ltd.	Beijing	http://www.huatai-serv.com/index.htm

5.2　Insurance agent

Article 117 of Insurance Law of the People's Republic of China states that insurance agents shall be institutions or individuals engaged by an insurer to handle insurance business on behalf of the insurer within the scope of the insurer's authorization and that charge a commission fee from the insurer. Insurance agencies include both dedicated insurance agencies that engage exclusively in insurance

---

① 開心保: http://www.kaixinbao.com/zixun/hangye/AG20130321017.shtml

agency business and non-dedicated insurance agencies that engage in insurance agency business as a sideline.

We can also say that an agent is one who acts for another. Insurance brokers bring insurance business for insurance companies.

The action of an insurance agent is looked upon the action of an insurer. If the insurance agent does insurance business on behalf of the insurer, he must be authorized and accredited by the insurance company. Besides what the insurance agent know is supposed to be known by the insurance company. Therefore insurance companies cannot refuse a claim because of the insured not performing the duty of disclosure.

Insurance agency must be in writing. This is because insurance agency is an important civil and legal action. The contract of an insurance agent should include the agent's name, contents, limit of authority, the period and the signature of the insurer and seal by the insurer. Insurance agents get commission from the insurer, for he acts for the insurer.

The insurer shall be held liable for the acts of its insurance agents when they transact insurance business on behalf of the insurance company in accordance with their delegated authority. Agents of insurance companies engaged in insurance of persons shall not accept delegation from more than one insurer concurrently.

Professional terms

insurance market	保險市場
Lloyd's market	勞合社市場
insurance organization	保險組織
insurance intermediary	保險中間人
actual or potential buyers	實際或潛在的購買者
strict definition	嚴格的定義
core of its activity	活動的核心
non-life insurance	非壽險
subscription market	認購市場
leading underwriter	首席承保人
write international business	承保國際業務
international market	國際保險市場
unique market	唯一的市場

in terms of geographical location	就地理位置而言
close vicinity	附近地區
underwriting capacity	承保能力
mode of operation	運行方式
potential new clients	潛在的新客戶
ancillary service	附加服務
loss adjusting	損失理算
transact insurance business	辦理保險業務
Department of Trade and Industry	貿工部
Insurance Companies Act	《保險公司法》
FTSE 100 Index	倫敦金融時報證券交易所 100 指數
fall into four groups	分為四類
the P & I clubs	保衛賠協會
Institute of London Underwriter, ILU	倫敦承保人協會
London Insurance and Reinsurance Market Association, LIRMA	倫敦保險與再保險市場協會
underwriting room	承保辦公室
short walking distance	短距離步行距離
geographical concentration of the market	市場的地理位置集中
Association of British Insurers, ABI	英國保險人協會
trade association	同業公會，行業協會
domestic insurance service	國內保險服務
major tax contributor	主要納稅貢獻者
British Insurance Association	英國保險人協會
Life Offices' Association	人壽保險協會
Accident Offices Association	意外保險協會
Industrial Life Offices Association	簡易人壽保險協會
Accident Offices Association (Overseas)	意外保險協會（海外）
main objective	主要目標
collective interests of the UK's insurance industry	英國保險業集體的利益
London market bureau	倫敦市場局
technical support	技術支持
London International Insurance and Reinsurance Market Association (LIRMA)	倫敦國際保險與再保險市場協會
a single voice	一個聲音
top priority	優先考慮的事，當務之急

replacement of out-of-date processes	更換過時的流程
London Market Group	倫敦市場集團
carrier's liability	承運人的責任
cargo-owner	貨主
ship-owner's liability	船主的責任
environmental pollution	環境污染
European Union Directive	《歐盟指引》
European Union	歐盟
maritime power	海洋大國
largest trading port	最大的貿易港口
Lloyd's of London	倫敦勞合社
Edward Lloyd	愛德華·勞埃德
Tower Street	塔街
Lloyd's building on Lime Street	位於石灰街的勞合社大樓
Corporation of Lloyd's Act	勞埃德公司法
pre-tax loss	稅前損失
annual level of claims for Lloyd's	勞埃德賠償的年度水平
pre-tax profit	稅前利潤
gross written premium	承保毛保險費
intermediary service	仲介服務
receive a commission	收到佣金
fringe company	周邊公司，邊緣公司
contact offices	聯絡處，辦事處
Marsh & McLennan Cos. Inc.	信達＆麥克倫南股份有限公司
public limited company P.L.C	公共有限公司，股份有限公司
Aon P. L. C.	怡安股份有限公司
Willis Group Holdings P.L.C.	威廉斯控股股份有限公司
Arthur J. Gallagher & Co.	亞瑟·J. 加拉格爾股份公司
Jardine Lloyd Thompson Group P.L.C.	賈丁·勞埃德·湯普森集團有限公司
BB & T Insurance Holdings Inc.	BB&T 保險控股有限公司
Wells Fargo Insurance Services USA Inc.	威爾斯·法戈保險服務美國有限公司
Hub International Ltd.	哈布國際有限公司
Lockton Cos. L. L. C.	洛克頓股份有限公司
China Insurance Regulatory Commission	中國保險監督委員會
Yingda Chang An Insurance Brokers Group Ldt.	英達長安保險經紀有限公司
Aon-COFCO Insurance Brokers Co., Ltd.	中怡保險經紀有限責任公司

Union Insurance Broker CO., Ltd.　　　北京聯合保險經紀有限公司
Jiang Tai Insurance Brokers Co., Ltd.　　江泰保險經紀有限公司
Marsh (Beijing) Insurance Brokers Co., Ltd.　　達信（北京）保險經紀有限公司
Willis Insurance Brokers Co., Ltd.　　韋萊（斯）保險經紀有限公司
Jing Sheng Insurance Brokers Co., Ltd.　　競盛保險經紀股份有限公司
Air Union Insurance Brokers Co,. Ltd.　　航聯保險經紀有限公司
Changcheng Insurance Brokers Company Ltd.　　長城保險經紀有限公司
Huatai Insurance Agency & Consultant Service Ltd.　　華泰保險經紀有限公司

Notes to the chapter

1. As for insurance market, however, there is no single place in the country or in a town where the buyers, sellers and middlemen meet to transact insurance.
然而，就保險市場而言，城鎮沒有一個單一的、買賣雙方以及中間人會面辦理保險業務的地方。

2. There is no strict definition of the term「London Insurance Market」. Some specialists believe that the core of its activity is the conduct of「internationally traded insurance and reinsurance business」.
對於「倫敦保險市場」這一術語沒有嚴格的定義。有些專家認為保險市場活動的核心是「進行全球性的保險和再保險業務的交易」

3. London insurance market is a「subscription market」in which insurances and reinsurances are placed by insurance brokers with two or more insurers or reinsurers who subscribe to a「slip」prepared by the broker.
倫敦保險市場是一個「認購市場」。在這個市場裡，保險經紀人準備好「承保單」，由兩個或兩個以上保險人或再保險人在「承保單」上認購。

4. The leading underwriter indicates the terms for acceptance of the business and each insurer states the share of the risk it is willing to accept on the slip.
首席承保人表明接受該業務的條款，然后各個保險人在承保單上確定願意承擔風險的份額。

5. London is unique market that is concentrated highly in terms of geographical location. It comprises a large number of insurers and intermediaries located in the City of London and its close vicinity.
在國際保險市場上，就地理位置而言，倫敦是唯一的一個高度集中的市場。

6. Which enables brokers to know personally the strengths, expertise and reputations of the underwriters and the insurers, and to gain access readily to the total market's underwriting capacity.

使保險經紀人能夠瞭解承保人和保險人的實力、專長以及聲譽,隨時獲取機會,瞭解整個市場的承保能力。

7. London's main attractions to foreign insurers and reinsurers to write international business are the mode of operation and reputation for innovation and security.

倫敦對外國保險人和再保險人承保國際業務的主要吸引力在於其運作模式、創新和安全的聲譽。

8. In 1983, the Departments of Trade and Industry were reunited. The Department of Energy was re-merged back into the DTI in 1992, but various media-related functions transferred to the Department for National Heritage. Until it was succeeded in June 2007, the DTI continued to set the energy policy of the United Kingdom.

1983 年,貿工部進行了重組。1992 年,能源部被並入貿工部,但是其他相關的職能轉入到國家文化遺產部。直到 2007 年 6 月,貿工部繼續負責制定英國的能源政策。

9. After the 2005 general election, the DTI was renamed to the Department for Productivity, Energy and Industry, but the name reverted to Department of Trade and Industry less than a week later.

2005 年大選之后,貿工部被更名為生產、能源和工業部,但是不到一個星期,又更名為貿工部。

10. A company wishing to transact insurance business in the UK must be licensed by the Department of Trade and Industry under the provisions of the Insurance Companies Act 1982.

凡是想在英國從事保險業務的公司必須按照 1982 年《保險公司法》的章程,並獲得由英國貿工部頒發的營業執照。

11. The advantages for brokers of this geographical concentration of the market have been reinforced by recent developments within the companies market.

市場的地理位置集中給經紀人帶來了好處,隨著近年來保險公司市場的發展,這種好處得到進一步強化。

12. Aviva has a primary listing on the London Stock Exchange and is a constituent of the FTSE 100 Index.

英杰華保險公司是倫敦股票交易所的主要上市公司,也是倫敦金融時報證券交易所 100 指數的組成部分。

13. RSA operates in 32 countries and provides insurance products and services in more than 140 through a global network of local partners.

RSA 在全球 32 個國家經營,通過當地合作夥伴的全球網絡,提供多達 140 項保險產品與服務。

14. Prudential's largest division is Prudential Corporation Asia, which has over 13 million customers across 12 Asian markets and is a top-three provider of life insurance in Hong Kong, India, Indonesia, Malaysia, Singapore, the Philippines and Vietnam.

保成最大的分公司是亞洲保成有限公司，在亞洲12個市場中擁有1300萬客戶，在香港、印度、印度尼西亞、馬來西亞、新加坡、菲律賓以及越南，是第三大壽險供應商。

15. ABI member companies account for almost 20 per cent of investments in London's stock market.

英國保險人協會的會員公司差不多占倫敦股票市場投資的20%。

16. The UK insurance industry is the largest in Europe and the third largest in the world.

英國保險行業在歐洲最大，在全世界排名第三。

17. The main objectives of ABI include the promotion of the interests of its members, and the representation of their views to the government and other agencies.

英國保險人協會的目標是提高會員的利益，向政府和其他機構表達他們的觀點。

18. It prepares a number of statistical and other publications, including an annual report, and consumer advice and crime prevention leaflets.

該協會準備許多統計數據和其他出版物，包括年度報告、消費者諮詢和犯罪預防的小冊子。

19. This business is wholesale, the bulk being made up of insurance for large multinational companies or reinsurance.

該業務是批發業務，大部分由大型的跨國公司或再保險公司承保。

20. The IUA provides a forum for discussing market issues and providing technical support to practitioners.

國際承保人協會舉辦一個論壇，討論市場關注的問題，並為從業者提供技術支持。

21. The main reason for the merger was the desire to give company market in London a single voice in dealings with government, regulators and other insurance bodies.

合併的主要原因是希望在同政府、監管者以及其他保險機構打交道時，倫敦保險公司市場發出一個聲音。

22. The association has always made reform of the London market a top priority, especially the replacement of out-of-date processes and increased use of technology to conduct business.

該協會優先考慮的事就是對倫敦市場進行了改革，特別是增加使用新的技術更換過時的流程。

23. The term「fringe companies」in the past referred to companies that operated on the fringes of the Lloyd's market.

「邊緣公司」過去指的是在勞合社市場附近運作的保險公司。

24. Normally they are relatively small companies which will take a small line on risks led by a Lloyd's syndicate.

一般說來，這些是相對較小的公司，接受由勞合社辛迪加分給他們很小的份額。

25. some foreign companies maintain an offer in London to keep in contact with the market, and to transmit to their head offices for acceptance any business which may be offered to them by brokers.

一些外資公司在倫敦設有一個窗口，以便保持與市場的聯繫，並把經紀人提供給的業務帶回到總公司承保。

26. Protection and indemnity insurance, more commonly known as P&I insurance, is a form of international maritime insurance provided by a P&I Club, a mutual insurance association that provides risk pooling, information and representation for its members, typically ship-owners and ship-operators.

保障與賠償保險，簡稱 P&I 保險，是由保障與賠償協會提供的國際海上保險業務。P&I 協會是一個相互保險協會，為會員提供風險集中、信息共享等。這些會員通常是船東和船舶營運者。

27. P&I clubs provide insurance for broader, indeterminate risks that marine insurers usually do not cover, such as third party risks.

P&I 協會提供更廣泛的、不確定的風險。這些風險通常是海上保險人不予承保的，比如第三者責任風險。

28. The European Union Directive was implemented in all 27 member States by January 1, 2012.

《歐盟指引》於 2012 年 1 月 1 日實施，其成員國有 27 個。

29. Foreign vessels that do not comply with the Directive will be expelled and refused entry into any EU port, although ships may be allowed some time to comply before expulsion.

雖然船舶有時可以容許進入歐盟港口，但是沒有遵守該指引的外國船舶將被驅逐或被拒絕進入歐盟任何港口。

30. Ever since the emergence of Britain as a maritime power and London as its largest trading port, Lloyd's of London has played the central role of a marine insurance market.

自從英國作為海洋大國、倫敦作為最大的貿易港口出現以來，倫敦勞合社在海上保險市場中發揮了重要的作用。

31. The capital which requires supporting the underwriting of insurances and reinsurances is supplied by investors, known as「Names」, who conduct their business through syndicates run by managing agents on the Names' behalf.

提供保險承保和再保險所需資金由稱之為「社員」的投資人提供，他們通過辛迪加承保業務，辛迪加由管理代理代表社員經營。

32. In 2011, over £23.44 billion of gross premiums were transacted in the Lloyd's market and in the aggregate it made a pre-tax loss of £516 million, driven by a number of significant natural disasters which gave rise to the highest ever annual level of claims for Lloyd's.

2011 年，勞合社市場交易的毛保險費超過 23.44 億英鎊，總計支付稅前賠償 5.16 億英鎊，這些賠償是由於重大自然災害造成的，是勞合社年度賠償最高紀錄。

Exercises

I. Questions

1. Give the definition of market.
2. What does the 「slip」 mean in the text?
3. Tell the features of London market.
4. Who regulates insurance company in UK?
5. What does the P & I club stand for?
6. What does the 「Names」 mean in the text?
7. What does insurance broker act as?
8. Can you briefly explain Lloyd's of London?

II. Find out a word in the text that means the same explanation and write down the word on the right column

1. A person who makes a purchase   1. _____
2. Living things and their activity   2. _____
3. Sign and accept liability under (an insurance policy), thus guaranteeing payment in case loss or damage occurs   3. _____
4. The area near or surrounding a particular place   4. _____
5. The capital of the United Kingdom, situated on the River Thames   5. _____
6. The length of the space between two points   6. _____
7. Goods carried on a ship, aircraft, or motor vehicle   7. _____
8. A sum, typically a set percentage of the value involved, paid to an agent in a commercial transaction   8. _____
9. A group of individuals or organizations combined to promote a common interest   9. _____
10. A group of people with the authority to govern a country or state   10. _____

III. True or false judgments

1. Some specialists believe that the core of its activity is the conduct of 「internationally traded insurance and reinsurance business」.   (   )

2. Among international markets, London is unique market that is concentrated highly in terms of economical location. (   )

3. A company wishing to transact insurance business in the UK must be licensed by the Association of British Insurers (ABI) under the provisions of the Insurance Companies Act 1985. (   )

4. Besides companies authorized to write insurance business in Britain, some foreign companies maintain an offer in London to keep in contact with the market, and to transmit to their head offices for acceptance any business which may be offered to them by brokers. (   )

5. Since the emergence of Britain as a maritime power and London as its largest trading port, Lloyd's of London has played the central role of a vessel insurance market. (   )

6. The IUA provides a forum for discussing market issues and providing technical support to practitioners. (   )

7. The main reason for the merger was the desire to give company market in London double voices in dealings with government, regulators and other insurance bodies. (   )

8. The association has always made reform of the London market a top priority, especially the replacement of update processes and increased use of technology to conduct business. (   )

9. The capital which requires supporting the underwriting of insurances and reinsurances is supplied by investors, known as Members, who conduct their business through syndicates run by managing agents on the Names' behalf. (   )

10. It is unnecessary for the insurer to be liable for the acts of its insurance agents when they transact insurance business on behalf of the insurance company in accordance with their delegated authority. (   )

Ⅳ. **Multiple choices**

1. London insurance market is a ⌈subscription market⌋ in which insurances and reinsurances are placed by insurance _____.

    A. brokers   B. agents   C. adjusters   D. assessors

2. Among international markets, _____ is unique market that is concentrated highly in terms of geographical location.

    A. New York   B. Paris   C. London   D. Beijing

3. A company wishing to transact insurance business in the UK must be _____ by the Department of Trade and Industry.

    A. licensed   B. allowed   C. permitted   D. agreed

4. The insurance and reinsurance companies operating in the London Market fall into _____ groups.

    A. three   B. two   C. four   D. five

5. Association of British Insurers (ABI) is the main trade association of insurance companies in the UK, it has around 300 companies in membership. ABI member companies account for almost _____ of investments in London's stock market.

  A. 50%   B. 30%   C. 70%   D. 20%

6. IUA represents companies that trade in the London insurance market outside Lloyd's. They wrote a total of at least _____ billion premiums during 2009, a figure that does not include income processed outside the London market bureau.

  A. £ 30   B. £ 100   C. £ 10   D. £ 20

7. The _____ was formed in January 1998 from the merger of the London International Insurance and Reinsurance Market Association (LIRMA) and the Institute of London Underwriters (ILU).

  A. IUA   B. ABI   C. DTI   D. IUAI

8. _____ in the past referred to companies that operated on the fringes of the Lloyd's market.

  A. Fringe companies   B. Contact offices
  C. Foreign companies   D. Lloyd's

9. Lloyd's of London has played the central role of a _____ insurance market.

  A. property   B. life   C. marine   D. motor

10. An insurance _____ means an entity or an individual, which has been delegated by an insurer and collects handling fees, to transact insurance business on behalf of the insurance company.

  A. adjustor   B. broker   C. assessor   D. agent

V. Translation from English to Chinese

1. The vast majority of commercial insurance will be transacted through a registered broker. In larger cases, these brokers will provide an in invaluable service to large corporations. Besides, the broker may also handle certain claims, draft policy wordings, carry out risk surveys, and provide risk management service and so on.

Brokers play a key role in bringing business to the insurance market. The insurance broker will choose a leading underwriter, who decides on the rate to be charged and conditions of the insurance and will assume the largest percentage of the risk. With the terms and conditions in place the slip will be taken to other insurers until 100% of the risk is placed after securing agreement from the insured.

2. Association of British Insurers (ABI) is the main trade association of insurance companies in the UK. According to the Association, it has around 300 companies in membership. Between them, they provide 90% of domestic insurance services sold in the UK. ABI member companies account for almost 20 per cent of investments in London's stock market. Its members are major tax contributors, paying £ 10.4 billion in the 2010/2011 tax year. The organization

is funded by members' subscriptions.

The main objectives of ABI include the promotion of the interests of its members, and the representation of their views to the government and other agencies. It prepares a number of statistical and other publications, including an annual report, and consumer advice and crime prevention leaflets.

Ⅵ. Translation from Chinese to English

1. 當我們談到市場時，會想到鄉鎮的週末市場。
2. 在國際市場上，就地理位置而言，倫敦是高度集中的保險市場。
3. 大多數保險公司既是國際承保人協會，同時也是英國保險人協會的會員。
4. 勞合社不是保險公司，而是一個保險市場。
5. 保險經紀人是中間人，在給倫敦市場帶來業務方面起著重要的作用。
6. 保險經紀人的手續費來自保險公司。
7. 保險代理人從保險人獲得手續費。
8. 保險代理人的行為被視為是保險人的行為。

Ⅶ. Case analysis

Tom owes ＄8,000 to his sister Catherine. In order to keep her loan in a safe position, Catherine wants to buy a life policy on Tom's life for ＄8,000. Five months later, Tom repays the loan ＄8,000 with the interest to Catherine. However, Catherine still maintains the life policy on Tom's life. Discuss what the position is upon Tom's death?

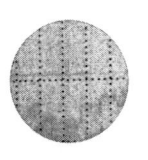

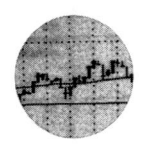

Chapter 8　**Structure of Insurance Company**

LEARNING OBJECTIVES:

☞ Learning about the structure of company
☞ Understanding the types of companies
☞ Learning about the structure of insurance company
☞ Learning about types of insurance company

CONTENTS OF THIS CHAPTER:

☞ Section 1 Structure of insurance company in China
☞ Section 2 Forms of insurance company in foreign countries
☞ Section 3 Insurance company as financial institute
☞ Section 4 Types of insurance company organizations

The purpose of a business as an organization is to produce goods or services for the consumers. If the consumers want these goods or services, then the business can sell those goods or services for a profit. It is important for an insurance company to have a responsibility to its owners to make profit in the insurance business.

Section 1 Structure of insurance company in China

Article 67 of Insurance Law of the People's Republic of China states that establishment of insurance companies shall be subject to the approval of the State Council's insurance regulatory authority. If you want to establish an insurance company, you should meet with the following conditions:

(1) the main shareholders having the capacity for sustained profitability, a good reputation, not having a record of a major violation of laws or regulations during the most recent three years and having net assets of not less than RMB 200 million;

(2) having articles of association in compliance with this Law and the PRC Company Law;

(3) having the registered capital as specified herein;

(4) having directors, supervisors and senior management personnel with the professional knowledge of their positions and work experience in the business;

(5) having a sound organizational structure and management system;

(6) having a place of business that meets the requirements, and having other business-related facilities;

(7) other conditions as specified by laws, administrative regulations or the State Council's insurance regulatory authority.

The minimum registered capital required for the establishment of an insurance company shall be RMB 200 million.[1] The State Council's insurance regulatory authority may, based on the scope of business and the size of insurance companies, adjust the minimum registered capital provided that the same is not lower than the limit specified in the first paragraph hereof. The registered capital of an insurance company must be paid-in monetary capital.[2] However, the minimum capital shall not be less than the amount stipulated in the insurance law.

After the application of the establishment of an insurance company has initially been reviewed and approved, the applicant shall begin preparing for the establishment of the insurance company in accordance with this Law and the Company Law.

1.1 The organizational structure of an insurance company

A solely state-owned insurance company shall have a Board of Supervisors, which comprises of representatives from the financial regulation agency and insurance regulatory authority, relevant experts, and employees of the insurance company.[3]

When an insurance company is unable to pay its debts when due, the insurance company can be declared bankrupt by the People's Court in accordance with laws. In the event that an insurance company is declared bankrupt, the People's Court shall appoint a liquidation task force that is composed of members from insurance regulatory authority and other relevant personnel to carry out the liquidation.

1.2 The major domestic insurance companies

China's first insurance company was established in Shanghai, 1875. It was called China Commercial Insurance Company. In 1876, the government of Qing dynasty ordered the Commercial Bureau to set up Renhe Insurance Company. This was the first insurance company established with national capital.

The foundation of People's Republic of China in 1949 marked the birthplace of New China. The development of New China's insurance industry began with the adjustment and alteration of the insurance industry and the insurance market in old China. The Central Government took over the insurance company set up by bureaucrat capital.

1.2.1 People's Insurance Company of China

Ratified by Financial Committee of the State Council, People's Insurance Company of China (PICC) was established in Beijing on October 20, 1949. The establishment of PICC marked the fast development of China's insurance industry.[4]

The development of China's insurance industry experienced both flourish and frustrations. Firstly, from the establishment to 1952, PICC made great development. But in 1953, rural insurance was cancelled and city business was adjusted. In 1958, all the internal insurance business was cancelled. In 1966, because of the「Cultural Revolution」, insurance was looked upon as feudalism, capitalism and revisionism. All the internal insurance business was almost cancelled.

In 1979, the national insurance business was restored and it was at this time that China's insurance industry entered a brand-new period.[5] Ratified by the State Council, PICC was reorganized and replaced by PICC (Group) in 1996, governing three subsidiary companies, namely, PICC (Property), PICC (Life) and PICC (Re).

After the reorganization, PICC Group made an outstanding achievement in the development in 1997. However, in 1998, in order to meet the need of the development in China's insurance industry, PICC Group was withdrawn and the original three subsidiary companies became independent state-owned insurance companies[6]: People's Insurance Company of China, China Life Insurance Company and China Reinsurance Company Limited. They have become state-owned corporate enterprises.

A historical event happened in PICC on 7th July 2003. The company was turned into a joint stock company with limited liability. It was called PICC Property and Casualty Company Limited. The People's Insurance Company of China was renewed and re-registered as PICC Holding Company. In November 6th 2003, it was successfully put into overseas market in the Stock Exchange of Hong Kong Limited.[7] PICC P&C has set up strategic partnership with American International Group, Inc. (AIG), who has purchased 9.9 percent of PICC's shares and would have long-term co-operations with PICC P&C in casualty and health insurance.

1.2.2 China Pacific Insurance Company

China Pacific Insurance Company (CPIC) which was developed during the spring tide of the reform and opening to the outside world. In 1986, the Communication Bank, after having stopped its business for 28 years, was reorganized. In 1987, the Communication Bank of China was authorized to set up the insurance business departments in its sub-branches of the different districts. In order to meet the need of the reform of our national financial system and the development of the insurance market, the People's Bank of China ratified the Communication Bank of China to set up a new insurance company. Based on its original insurance business, the new insurance company was formally named as 「the China Pacific Insurance Company」. On April 26th, 1991, the company opened business officially in Shanghai. Ever since then, the insurance businesses in the Communication Bank of China had been transferred to the China Pacific Insurance Company. From the beginning of 1991 to the end of 1996, CPIC had become a nationwide joint-stock company, with more than 60 sub-branches in China and two subsidiaries overseas.

1.2.3　Ping An Insurance Company Of China

Ping An Insurance Company Of China (PAICC) is the first joint-stock enterprise. It was established in Shenzhen, Guangdong province in March 1988. The major stockholders are Shenzhen Commercial Bureau, the Industrial & Commercial Bank of China, China Ocean Shipping Company and the Financial Bureau of Shenzhen city,[8] with the registered capital of 300 million Yuan. Soon the increase of capital and the extension of stock shares have reached 1,000 million Yuan. On September 1992, PAICC, authorized by People's Bank of China, opened its business throughout China. Since then, PAICC became the third national insurance company from the regional insurance company and was allowed to handle all risks and international reinsurance business. In 1994, it became the second largest insurance company in China.

In addition, there were many smaller insurance companies established in recent years, including New China Life Insurance Company, Ltd. Tai Kang Life Insurance Company, Ltd. China United Insurance Company, Ltd. Sino-safe General Insurance Company, Ltd. Yong An Property Insurance Company, Ltd. Tian An Insurance Company Limited of China, Hua Tai Insurance Company of China, Ltd. and Da Zhong Insurance Company, Ltd. and so on. Most of them have become nationwide insurance companies. It is reported that there are 128 insurance companies in 2013, including property insurances and life insurances.

Section 2   Forms of insurance company in foreign countries

Each business organization is structured in one of three ways: a sole proprietorship, a partnership or a corporation.

2.1   Sole proprietorship

A sole proprietorship is owned and operated by one individual.[9] The owner reaps all profits and is responsible for all the debts of the business. The size of the business is limited by the amount of money that the owner can personally raise.[10] If the business fails, the owner's personal property may be used to satisfy the debts of the business.[11] If the owner becomes disabled or dies, the business usually closes its doors. Before he becomes disabled or dies, he can leave the assets and liabilities of the business to someone else to continue the operation of a sole proprietorship.

2.2   Partnership

A partnership is a business that is co-owned by two or more people.[12] They are known as the partners. Each partner is responsible for the debts of the whole business, not just for a proportionate share based on that partner's original investment in the business. The partners reap the profits and are personally responsible for the debts of the business. An unwise decision by one partner can endanger the personal funds of all other partners.[13] If one of the partners dies or withdraws from the business, the partnership generally dissolves, although the remaining partners may form a new partnership.

2.3   Corporation

A corporation is a legal entity created by the authority of a government.[14] A corporation has two major characteristics that set it apart from a sole proprietorship and a partnership.[15]

Firstly, a corporation is a legal entity that is separate from its owners. As a result, a corporation can sue or be sued, can enter into contracts, and can own property. The corporation's debts and liabilities belong to the corporation itself, not to its owners. Therefore the owners are not personally responsible for the corporation's debts.

Secondly the other difference is that the corporation continues even if any or all of its owners die. This second characteristic of the corporation provides stability and permanence that a sole proprietorship and partnership cannot guarantee.[16] It is this stability that makes the corporation the ideal form of business organization for an insurance company.

Furthermore, a corporation is well managed and can survive the personal misfortunes of any of its owners.[17] People possibly make an investment in the corporation and buy its products. Because insurance companies must be permanent and stable organizations, laws in the many western countries, especially in United States and Canada require insurance companies to operate as corporations.

Section 3 Insurance companies as financial institutions

Within each geographic region, a company may have field offices. A field office is an insurance company's local sales office out of which its field forces or sales agents work.[18] The home office and regional office typically provide support services to the field office.[19] Some field offices are classified as branch offices while others are classified as agency offices. It all depends on how they are organized and what the working relationship is with the home office.

These structural aspects of insurance organizations vary widely from one company to another, which depends on the size of the company's operations and the geographic markets it serves.

3.1 Financial service industry

Insurance companies are financial institutions that function as part of the financial service industry in the economy.[20] A financial institution is an organization that helps to channel funds through an economy by accepting the surplus money of savers and supplying that money to borrowers who pay to use the money.[21] The financial services industry is made up of financial institutions that help consumers and business organizations save, borrow, invest and manage money.

Insurance companies are among the most important financial institutions in North America. They make a significant contribution to the economic growth, both as investors in their economies and as employers. Life and health insurance companies invest their assets in other businesses and industries as well as in mortgage loans. These investments help provide the funds that other businesses need to operate and grow and that individuals need to purchase homes. The life and health insurance industry is also a major employer in western countries. For example, United States and Canada employ several million people to engage in life insurance business.

In addition to providing funds for economic growth, insurance companies also invest in social programs that help improve the quality of life for all people. For example, life and health insurance companies invest money to further AIDS research and education and to provide support to charitable organizations.

The financial services industry has undergone profound changes in the past few decades. Various types of financial institutions provided financial services, and the activities of each type of financial institution were distinct. In fact, legal restrictions separated the activities of financial institutions. Banks, as well as U. S. savings and loan institutions and Canadian trust companies, accepted customer deposits and made consumer loans. Investment companies offered investment products. Insurance companies provided insurance products.[22]

3.2 The mixture of financial institutions

Today, however, the distinctions between these financial institutions have become more and more confusable. In Canada and the United States, laws have been changed so that each type of financial institution can now offer a wider variety of products.[23] Banks now may offer investment products and insurance products, in addition to the usual checking and savings accounts. Insurance companies have begun to offer a wider variety of insurance, as well as non-insurance products, such as savings plans, mortgage loans, and mutual funds. In short, financial institutions are competing with one another to provide a wide range of financial services to today's sophisticated consumers.

Section 4 Types of insurance company organizations

Even though they must be corporations, life and health insurance companies have some flexibility in how they are organized to do business. Most insurance companies are organized as either stock companies or mutual companies.

4.1 Stock insurance companies

The majority of life and health insurance companies are established and organized as stock companies. A stock insurance company is formed as a corporation. The funds that the corporation needs to begin operations come from investors who purchase stock-ownership shares in the corporation.[24] The individuals who hold shares of stock in the company, known as the stockholders, then, own a stock company. From time to time, a portion of the company's operating profits may be distributed to these stockholders in the form of stockholder dividends.

4.2 Mutual insurance companies

A mutual insurance company is owned by its policy-owners and a portion of the company's operating profits are from time to time distributed to these policy-owners.[25] When profits are distributed to the owners of a mutual company, they are distributed in the form of policy dividends.

Before a mutual company can be formed, a certain number of policies must be sold in advance to provide the funds the company needs to begin operations.[26] Because most people are reluctant to purchase a product from a company that does not yet exist, most mutual companies begin as stock companies and later convert to mutual companies. This process of converting from a stock company to a mutual company is called mutualization.[27]

Mutual companies can be demutualized and be reorganized as stock companies.[28] The reason why a mutual insurer might wish to demutualize is that it can more easily raise operating funds, for it can sell shares of stock. Stock insurers also have greater flexibility than mutual insurers in buying and operating other types of companies. In today's highly competitive financial services marketplace, some mutual insurers are reorganizing as stock companies in order to enhance their ability to raise capital and to enable them to purchase other organizations.[29]

Even though stock insurers greatly outnumber mutual insurers, mutual insurers provide a significant amount of the life insurance in force in United States and Canada.[30] Mutual insurers account for a significant amount of life insurance in force because they are generally older and larger than stock insurers.[31]

Professional terms

structure of company	公司結構
financial institute	金融機構
stock company	股份公司
limited liability	有限責任
sole state-owned enterprise	國有獨資企業
articles of corporation	公司章程
establishment of an insurance company	保險公司的建立
registered capital	註冊資本

financial regulation authority	金融監管部門
solely state-owned insurance company	國有獨資保險公司
Board of Supervisors	監事會
minimum solvency margin	最低償付能力
state-owned asset	國有資產
liquidation task force	清算組，清算團隊
violation of law	違反法律
administrative regulation	行政管理
government of Qing dynasty	清政府
Renhe Insurance Company	仁和保險公司
bureaucrat capital	官僚資本
Financial Committee of the State Council	國務院財經委員會
rural insurance	地方保險
Cultural Revolution	文化大革命
a brand-new period	全新的時代
subsidiary company	子公司
outstanding achievement	傑出的成績
joint stock company	股份公司
PICC Holding Company	中國人民保險控股公司
Stock Exchange of Hong Kong Limited	香港股票交易有限公司
strategic partnership	戰略合夥人
American International Group, Inc.	美國國際保險集團
China Pacific Insurance Company	中國太平洋保險公司
Communication Bank of China	中國交通銀行
Ping An Insurance Company of China	中國平安保險公司
Industrial & Commercial Bank of China	中國工商銀行
Shenzhen Commercial Bureau	深圳招商局
China Ocean Shipping Company	中國海洋運輸公司
Financial Bureau of Shenzhen city	深圳市財政局
New China Life Insurance Company, Ltd.	新華人壽保險有限公司
Tai Kang Life Insurance Company, Ltd.	泰康人壽保險有限公司
China United Insurance Company, Ltd.	中華聯合保險有限公司
Sino-safe General Insurance Company, Ltd.	華安財產保險有限公司
Yong An Property Insurance Company, Ltd.	永安財產保險有限公司
Tian An Insurance Company Limited of China	天安保險有限公司
Hua Tai Insurance Company of China, Ltd.	華泰保險有限公司

Da Zhong Insurance Company, Ltd.	大眾保險有限公司
sole proprietorship	獨資企業
new partnership	新的合夥人
corporation's debts and liabilities	公司的債務和責任
stability and permanence	穩定與永久性
permanent and stable organization	永久和穩定的組織
field office	外地辦公室
local sales office	當地銷售辦公室
home office	總店，總公司
agency office	代理辦公室
financial service industry	金融服務行業
economic growth	經濟增長
mortgage loan	抵押貸款
life and health insurance industry	人壽和健康保險行業
social program	社會事業
further AIDS research	更深層次的愛滋病研究
charitable organization	慈善組織
checking and savings account	支票和儲蓄帳戶
non-insurance product	非壽險產品
savings plan	儲蓄計劃
mutual fund	共同基金
sophisticated consumer	有經驗的消費者
mutual company	相互公司
stockholder dividend	股票持有人紅利
mutual insurance company	相互保險公司
policy-owner	保單所有者
policy dividend	保單紅利
process of mutualization	股份公司相互化的過程
competitive financial services marketplace	競爭的金融服務市場
raise operating fund	籌集運作基金
raise capital	籌集資金
mutual insurers	相互保險人

Notes to the chapter

1. The minimum amount of registered capital required for the establishment of an insurance company shall be RMB 200 million.

設立保險公司，其註冊資本的最低限額為人民幣 2 億元。

2. The State Council's insurance regulatory authority may, based on the scope of business and the size of insurance companies, adjust the minimum registered capital provided that the same is not lower than the limit specified in the first paragraph hereof. The registered capital of an insurance company must be paid-in monetary capital.

國務院保險監督管理機構根據保險公司的業務範圍、經營規模，可以調整其註冊資本的最低限額，但不得低於本條第一款規定的限額。保險公司的註冊資本必須為實繳貨幣資本。

3. A solely state-owned insurance company shall have a Board of Supervisors, which comprises of representatives from the financial regulation authority, relevant experts, and employees of the insurance company.

獨資國有保險公司設立監事會，監事會由金融監管部門、相關專家以及保險公司的雇員組成。

4. The establishment of PICC marked the fast development of China's insurance industry.

中國人民保險公司的建立標誌著中國保險業的快速發展。

5. In 1979, the national insurance business was restored and it was at this time that China's insurance industry entered a brand-new period.

1979 年，國內保險業務得到恢復，就是在這個時候，中國的保險業進入了全新的時代。

6. However, in 1998, in order to meet the need of the development in China's insurance industry, PICC Group was withdrawn and the original three subsidiary companies became independent state-owned insurance companies:

然而 1988 年，為了滿足中國保險業發展的需要，中國人民保險集團被撤銷，原來的三家子公司成為獨立的國有保險公司。

7. In November 6th 2003, it was successfully put into overseas market in the Stock Exchange of Hong Kong Limited.

2003 年 11 月 6 日，該公司在海外市場香港聯交所上市。

8. The major stockholders are Shenzhen Commercial Bureau, the Industrial & Commercial Bank of China, China Ocean Shipping Company and the Financial Bureau of Shenzhen city.

主要股東是深圳招商局、中國工商銀行、中國海洋運輸公司以及深圳市財政局。

9. A sole proprietorship is owned and operated by one individual.

獨資企業是指由一個人擁有和經營的企業。

10. The size of the business is limited by the amount of money that the owner can personally raise.

企業的規模大小受到個人籌資數量多少的限制。

11. If the business fails, the owner's personal property may be used to satisfy the debts of the business.

如果獨資企業經營失敗，業主的個人財產將被用來償還企業的債務。

12. A partnership is a business that is co-owned by two or more people.

合夥企業是由兩個或兩個以上人員共同擁有的企業。

13. An unwise decision by one partner can endanger the personal funds of all other partners.

一個合夥人不明智的決定將傷害所有其他合夥人的資金。

14. A corporation is a legal entity created by the authority of a government.

法人公司是指由政府授權建立的法人實體。

15. A corporation has two major characteristics that set it apart from a sole proprietorship and a partnership.

法人公司有兩個主要的特點與獨資企業和合夥企業不同。

16. This second characteristic of the corporation provides stability and permanence that a sole proprietorship and partnership cannot guarantee.

法人公司的第二個特點是具有穩定性和持續性，而獨資企業和合夥企業則不能保障其穩定性和持續性。

17. Furthermore, a corporation is well managed and can survive the personal misfortunes of any of its owners.

此外，法人公司能夠進行很好的管理，能夠從任何所有者的不幸遭遇中生存下來。

18. A field office is an insurance company's local sales office out of which its field forces or sales agents work.

「field office」指的是保險公司當地銷售辦公室，是銷售人員和銷售代理人工作的地方。

19. The home office and regional office typically provide support services to the field office.

總公司和區域公司為當地銷售辦公室提供服務支持。

20. Insurance companies are financial institutions that function as part of the financial service industry in the economy.

保險公司是金融機構，其功能就是金融服務行業經濟的一部分。

21. A financial institution is an organization that helps to channel funds through an econ-

omy by accepting the surplus money of savers and supplying that money to borrowers who pay to use the money.

金融機構是通過經濟手段幫助融資的一個組織，接受儲戶的剩余資金，並將其貸給交納利息的借款人。

22. In fact, legal restrictions separated the activities of financial institutions. Banks, as well as U. S. savings and loan institutions and Canadian trust companies, accepted customer deposits and made consumer loans. Investment companies offered investment products. Insurance companies provided insurance products.

事實上，法律限定分離了金融機構的活動。銀行、美國儲蓄與貸款機構以及加拿大信託公司接受客戶的存款，然后向客戶發放貸款。投資公司提供投資產品，保險公司提供保險產品。

23. Today, however, the distinctions between these financial institutions have become more and more confusable. In Canada and the United States, laws have been changed so that each type of financial institution can now offer a wider variety of products.

然而今天，這些金融機構之間的區分變得越來越模糊，在加拿大和美國，法律已經發生了變化，各種金融機構現在都可以提供更廣泛的各種金融產品。

24. The funds that the corporation needs to begin operations come from investors who purchase stock-ownership shares in the corporation.

公司所需啓動資金來自於投資者購買公司的股權份額。

25. A mutual insurance company is owned by its policy-owners and a portion of the company's operating profits are from time to time distributed to these policy-owners.

相互保險公司由保單持有人共同所有，公司所獲得的利潤不時地分發給保單持有人。

26. Before a mutual company can be formed, a certain number of policies must be sold in advance to provide the funds the company needs to begin operations.

相互保險公司建立之前，要提前出售一定數量的保險單，以便提供公司需要的啓動資金。

27. This process of converting from a stock company to a mutual company is called mutualization.

從股份公司轉換成相互公司的過程稱之為股份公司相互化。

28. Mutual companies can be demutualized and be reorganized as stock companies.

相互保險公司能夠進行股份制改造，重新組建成股份公司。

29. In today's highly competitive financial services marketplace, some mutual insurers are reorganizing as stock companies in order to enhance their ability to raise capital and to enable them to purchase other organizations.

在今天高度競爭的金融服務市場，一些相互保險公司重新構建成股份公司，以便

提供他們的融資能力，購買其他組織。

30. Even though stock insurers greatly outnumber mutual insurers, mutual insurers provide a significant amount of the life insurance in force in United States and Canada.

在西方國家，雖然股份保險公司的數量大大超過相互公司，但是相互保險公司提供的壽險業務總量非常巨大。

31. Mutual insurers account for a significant amount of life insurance in force because they are generally older and larger than stock insurers.

相互保險公司之所以佔有效壽險巨大的業務總量，是因為相互保險公司的歷史比股份公司要長，其規模也比股份公司要大。

Exercises

Ⅰ. Questions

1. Explain the purpose of a business as an organization.
2. What does a sole proprietorship mean?
3. Can you explain what a partnership is?
4. What is the definition of a corporation?
5. Tell the major stockholders of Ping An Insurance Company.
6. Tell the difference between a field office and a home office.
7. What is a stock insurance company?
8. What is a mutual insurance company?

Ⅱ. Match up the explanations of the left column with the word on the right column

1. The least or smallest amount or quantity possible, or required
2. The action of violating someone or something
3. A group of people appointed for a specific function by a larger group and typically consisting of members of that group
4. A thing done successfully with effort, skill, or courage
5. The means of travelling or of transporting goods, such as roads or railways
6. Economic activity concerned with the processing of raw materials and manufacture of goods in factories
7. The activity of buying and selling, especially on a large scale

1. committee (　　)
2. commerce (　　)
3. research (　　)
4. dividend (　　)
5. fund (　　)
6. violation (　　)
7. industry (　　)

8. A sum of money paid regularly (typically annually) by a company to its shareholders out of its profits or reserves   8. minimum ( )

9. The systematic investigation into and study of materials and sources in order to establish facts and reach new conclusions   9. communication ( )

10. A sum of money saved or made available for a particular purpose   10. achievement ( )

Ⅲ. True or false judgments

1. Each business organization is structured in one of three ways: a sole proprietorship, a partnership or a business. ( )

2. The establishment of CPIC marked the fast development of China's insurance industry. ( )

3. A sole proprietorship is owned and operated by one individual. A partnership is a business that is co-owned by two or more people. ( )

4. A corporation is a legal entity created by the authority of a government. ( )

5. Insurance companies are financial institutions that function in the economy as part of the financial Services industry. ( )

6. The financial services industry has undergone profound changes in the past few decades. ( )

7. The minority of life and health insurance companies are established and organized as stock companies. ( )

8. A mutual insurance company is an insurance company that is owned by its policy-owners, and a portion of the company's operating profits are from time to time distributed to these policy-owners. ( )

9. Mutual companies can be mutualized and be reorganized as stock companies. ( )

10. Mutual insurers account for a significant amount of life insurance in force because they are generally younger and smaller than stock insurers. ( )

Ⅳ. Multiple choices

1. _____ is the money that a business receives for its products or services minus the costs it incurred to produce the goods or deliver the services.

     A. Benefit   B. Expense   C. Commission   D. Profit

2. A sole proprietorship is owned and operated by _____. The owner reaps all profits and is responsible for all the debts of the business.

     A. one individual   B. individuals   C. members   D. two people

3. A _____ is a business that is co-owned by two or more people.

   A. sole proprietorship   B. corporation

   C. partnership   D. company

4. A corporation is a legal entity created by the authority of a(n) _____.

   A. applicant   B. broker   C. insurer   D. government

5. A(n) _____ is an insurance company's local sales office out of which its field forces or sales agents work.

   A. head office   B. field office   C. institution   D. regional office

6. Today, however, the distinctions between these financial institutions have become more and more _____.

   A. clear   B. obvious   C. confusable   D. definite

7. The majority of life and health insurance companies are established and organized as _____ in USA.

   A. mutual companies   B. stock companies

   C. state-owned companies   D. private companies

8. Before a mutual company can be formed, a certain number of _____ must be sold in advance to provide the funds the company needs to begin operations.

   A. policies   B. properties   C. houses   D. offices

9. A mutual insurance company is an insurance company that is owned by its _____.

   A. policy-owners   B. shareholders   C. stockholders   D. employers

10. Mutual insurers account for a significant amount of life insurance in force because they are generally _____ than stock insurers.

    A. newer and smaller   B. older and larger

    C. newer and larger   D. smaller and older

V. Translation from English to Chinese

1. The minimum amount of registered capital required for the establishment of an insurance company shall be RMB 200 million. The minimum amount of registered capital for the establishment of an insurance company shall be fully paid-up in monetary form. The financial regulation authority and regulatory authority may adjust the amount of the minimum registered capital, in accordance with the proposed scope of business and scale of operations; however, the minimum capital shall not be less than the amount stipulated in the insurance law.

2. Insurance companies are financial institutions that function in the economy as part of the financial Services industry. A financial institution is an organization that helps to channel funds through an economy by accepting the surplus money of savers and supplying that money to borrowers who pay to use the money. The financial services industry is made up of financial institutions that help consumers and business organizations save, borrow, invest and manage

money.

In addition to providing funds for economic growth, insurance companies also invest in social programs that help improve the quality of life for all people. For example, life and health insurance companies invest money to further AIDS research and education and to provide support to charitable organizations.

Ⅵ. Translation from Chinese to English

1. 中國第一家保險公司於 1875 年在上海成立。
2. 中國人民保險公司的建立標誌著中國保險業的快速發展。
3. 法人公司是指由政府授權建立的法人實體。
4. 如果這個業主殘疾或去世了，企業通常就關門了。
5. 法人公司的債務和責任屬於公司本身，不屬於所有者。
6. 在西方國家，特別是在北美，保險公司是最重要的金融機構。
7. 區分保險公司和銀行的職能變得越來越模糊。
8. 相互保險公司能夠被轉發為股份公司。

Ⅶ. Case analysis

When Mr. Smith visited the offices of Moon Insurance Company, he picked up a prospectus for motor insurance. He calculated the premium for his own car with the insurance rate which was quoted on the prospectus. The next day he posted the proposal form as well as the prospectus to the insurance company. At the same time he also posted the premium $1,500 to the insurance company, asking the insurance company to accept the cover immediately. Five days later, his car was destroyed by fire. However the insurance company has not dealt with the proposal form because it was put into the tray on a clerk's desk.

Do you think Mr. Smith can be indemnified by Moon Insurance Company? Give your analysis.

Appendix I
OCEAN MARINE CARGO CLAUSES

(1/1/1981)

I. Scope of Cover

This insurance is classified into the following three Conditions-Free from Particular Average (F. P. A.), With Average (W. A.) and All Risks. Where the goods insured hereunder sustain loss or damage, the Company shall undertake to indemnify therefor according to the Insured Condition specified in the Policy and the Provisions of these Clauses:

(1) Free From Particular Average (F. P. A.). This insurance covers:

Total or Constructive Total Loss of the whole consignment hereby insured caused in the course of transit by natural calamities-heavy weather, lightning, tsunami, earthquake and flood. In case a constructive total loss is claimed for, the Insured shall abandon to the Company the damaged goods and all his rights and title pertaining thereto. The goods on each lighter to or from the seagoing vessel shall be deemed a separate risk.

「Constructive Total Loss」refers to the loss where an actual total loss appears to be unavoidable or the cost to be incurred in recovering or reconditioning the goods together with the forwarding cost to the destination named in the Policy would exceed their value on arrival.

Total or Partial Loss caused by accidents -the carrying conveyance being grounded, stranded, sunk or in collision with floating ice or other objects as fire or explosion.

Partial loss of the insured goods attributable to heavy weather, lightning and/or tsunami, where the conveyance has been grounded, stranded, sunk or burnt, irrespective of whether the event or events took place before or after such accidents.

Partial or total loss consequent on falling of entire package or packages into sea during loading, transhipment or discharge.

Reasonable cost incurred by the Insured in salvaging the goods or averting or minimizing a loss recoverable under the Policy, provided that such cost shall not exceed the sum Insured of the consignment so saved.

Losses attributable to discharge of the insured goods at a port of distress following a sea peril as well as special charges arising from loading, warehousing and forwarding of the goods at an intermediate port of call or refuge.

Sacrifice in and Contribution to General Average and Salvage Charges.

Such proportion of losses sustained by the shipowners as is to be reimbursed by the Cargo Owner under the Contract of Affreightment 「Both to Blame Collision」clause.

(2) With Particular Average (W. P. A.). Aside from the risks covered under F. P. A. Condition as above, this insurance also covers partial losses of the insured goods caused by heavy weather, lightning, tsunami, earthquake and/or flood.

(3) All Risks. Aside from the risks covered under the F. P. A and W. A. Conditions as above, this insurance also covers all risks of loss of or damage to the insured goods whither partial or total, arising from external causes in the course of transit.

II. Exclusions

This Insurance does not cover:

(1) Loss or damage caused by the intentional act or fault of the Insured.

(2) Loss or damage falling under the liability of the consignor.

(3) Loss or damage arising from the inferior quality or shortage of the insured goods prior to the attachment of this insurance.

(4) Loss or damage arising from normal loss, inherent vice or nature of the insured goods, loss of market and/or delay in transit and any expenses arising therefrom.

(5) Risks and liabilities covered and excluded by the Ocean Marine Cargo War Risks Clauses and Strike, Riot and Civil Commotion Clauses of this company.

III. Commencement and Termination of Cover

(1) Warehouse to Warehouse Clause:

This insurance attaches from the time the goods hereby insured leave the warehouse or place of storage named in the Policy for the commencement of the transit and continues in force in the ordinary course of transit including sea, land and inland waterway transits and transit in lighter until the insured goods are delivered to the consignee's final warehouse or place or storage at the destination named in the Policy or to any other place used by the Insured for allocation or distribution of the goods or for storage other than in the ordinary course of transit. This insurance shall, however, be limited to sixty (60) days after completion of discharge of the insured goods from the seagoing vessel at the final port of discharge before they reach the above mentioned warehouse or place of storage. If prior to the expiry of the above mentioned sixty (60) days, the insured goods are to be forwarded to a destination other than that named in the Policy, this insurance shall terminate at the commencement of such transit.

(2) If, owing to delay, deviation, forced discharge, reshipment or transhipment beyond the control of the Insured or any change or termination of the voyage arising from the exercise of a liberty granted to the shipowners under the contract of affreightment, the insured goods arrive at a port or place other than that named in the Policy, subject to immediate notice being given to the Company by the Insured and an additional premium being paid, if required, this insurance shall remain in force and shall terminate as hereunder:

If he insured goods are sold at port or place not named in the Policy, this insurance shall terminate on delivery of the goods sold, but in no event shall this insurance extend beyond sixty (60) days after completion of discharge of the insured goods from the carrying vessel at such port or place.

If the insured goods are to be forwarded to the final destination named in the Policy or any other destination, this insurance shall terminate in accordance with Section 1 above.

IV. **Duty of the Insured**

It is the duty of the Insured to attend to all matters as specified hereunder, failing which the Company reserves the right to reject his claim for any loss if and when such failure prejudice the rights of the Company:

(1) The Insured shall take delivery of the insured goods in good time upon their arrival at the port of destination named in the Policy. In the event of any damage to the goods, the Insured shall immediately apply for survey to the survey and/or settling agent stipulated in the Policy. If the insured goods are found short in entire package or packages or to show apparent traces of damage, the Insured shall obtain from the carrier, bailee or other relevant authorities (Customs and Port Authorities etc.) certificate of loss or damage and/or short landed memo. Should the carrier, bailee or the other relevant authorities be responsible for such shortage or damage, the Insured shall lodge a claim with them in writing and, if necessary, obtain their confirmation of an extension of the time limit of validity of such claim.

(2) The Insured shall, and the Company may also, take reasonable measures immediately in salvaging the goods or preventing or minimizing a loss or damage thereto. The measures so taken by the Insured or by the Company shall not be considered respectively, as a waiver of abandonment hereunder, or as an acceptance thereof.

(3) In case of a change of voyage or any omission or error in the description of the interest, the name of the vessel or voyage, this insurance shall remain in force only upon prompt notice to this Company when the Insured becomes aware of the same and payment of an additional premium if required.

(4) The following documents should accompany any claim hereunder made against this Company:

Original Policy, Bill of Lading, Invoice, Packing List, Tally Sheet, Weight Memo, Certificate of Loss or Damage and/or Short landed Memo, Survey Report, and Statement of Claim.

If any third party is involved, documents relative to pursuing of recovery from such party should also be included.

(5) Immediate notice should be given to the Company when the Cargo Owner's actual responsibility under the contract of affreightment「Both to Blame Collision」clause becomes known.

V. The Time of Validity of a Claim

The time of validity of a claim under this insurance shall not exceed a period of two years counting from the time of completion of discharge of the insured goods from the seagoing vessel at the final port of discharge.

Appendix Ⅱ Insurance Law of the People's Republic of China in 2009 (Amended)

Chapter Ⅰ General Provisions ·············· 156

Chapter Ⅱ Insurance Contract ·············· 157

    Section 1 General Provisions ·············· 157

    Section 2 Personal Insurance Contract ·············· 162

    Section 3 Property Insurance Contract ·············· 165

Chapter Ⅲ Insurance Companies ·············· 169

Chapter Ⅳ Insurance Business Rules ·············· 174

Chapter Ⅴ Insurance Agents and Insurance Brokerages ·············· 179

Chapter Ⅵ Oversight of the Insurance Industry ·············· 181

Chapter Ⅶ Legal Liability ·············· 186

Chapter Ⅷ Supplementary Provisions ·············· 191

Chapter I   General Provisions

Article 1   This Law has been formulated to regulate insurance activities, protect the lawful rights and interests of the parties to insurance activities, strengthen the supervision and administration over the insurance industry, maintain the order of the society and economy, safeguard the public interest and promote the healthy development of the insurance business.

Article 2   For the purposes of this Law, the term 「insurance」 means the commercial insurance act whereby the proposer pays insurance premiums to the insurer in accordance with the contract and the insurer is liable for payment of indemnities in connection with property losses arising due to the occurrence of an event the possibility of the occurrence of which is specified in the contract; or the insurer is liable for payment of insurance benefits due to the death, injury, disability or illness of the insured, or conditions such as age and term specified in the contract being satisfied.

Article 3   This Law shall apply to all insurance activities engaged in within the People's Republic of China.

Article 4   Parties engaging in insurance activities must obey laws and administrative regulations, defer to the norms of social ethics, and may not harm the public interest.

Article 5   The parties to insurance activities shall abide by the principle of good faith when exercising their rights and performing their obligations.

Article 6   Insurance business shall be engaged in by insurance companies established in accordance with this Law and other insurance organizations specified in laws and administrative regulations. Other work units and individuals may not engage in insurance business.

Article 7   Legal persons and other organizations in the People's Republic of China that need to take out domestic insurance policies shall do so with insurance companies in the People's Republic of China.

Article 8   Insurance business shall be engaged in and managed separately from banking, securities or trust business, and insurance companies and banking, securities or trust business institutions shall be established separately, unless otherwise provided by the state.

Article 9   The State Council's insurance regulatory authority shall regulate the insurance business in accordance with the law.

The State Council's insurance regulatory authority shall establish agencies as required for the performance of its duties. An agency shall perform its regulatory duties as authorized by the State Council's insurance regulatory authority.

Chapter Ⅱ Insurance Contract

Section 1 General Provisions

Article 10 An insurance contract is an agreement in which a proposer and an insurer stipulate their respective obligations and rights in respect of an insurance policy.

The term 「proposer」 refers to the party that concludes an insurance contract with the insurer and bears the obligation to pay insurance premiums in accordance with the contract.

The term 「insurer」 refers to the insurance company that concludes an insurance contract with a proposer and is liable for payment of insurance indemnities or benefits in accordance with the contract.

Article 11 To conclude an insurance contract, the parties shall reach agreement through consultations and determine their respective rights and obligations based on the principle of fairness. Except where laws and administrative regulations require that insurance be taken out, insurance contracts shall be concluded by the parties of their own free will.

Article 12 When concluding a personal insurance contract, the proposer shall have an insurable interest in the insured.

The insured under property insurance shall, when an insured event occurs, have an insurable interest in the subject matter of insurance.

Personal insurance is insurance under which the subject matter of insurance is the life and body of a person.

Property insurance is insurance under which the subject matter of insurance is property and related interests therein.

The term 「insured」 means the person whose property or whose own person is protected by the insurance contract and who has the right to claim insurance proceeds. The proposer may be the insured. The term 「insurable interest」 means the legally recognized interest that the proposer or insured has in the subject matter of insurance.

Article 13 An insurance contract shall be formed when a proposer makes a request for insurance and the insurer agrees to insure. The insurer shall issue the proposer an insurance policy document or other insurance certificate in a timely manner.

The insurance policy document or other insurance certificate shall specify the contractual terms agreed upon by the parties. The parties may agree to adopt another written form to specify the contractual terms.

A lawfully formed insurance contract shall enter into effect once it is formed. The proposer and insurer may agree to attach conditions to, or specify a period of time for, the validity of the contract.

Article 14   Once an insurance contract has been formed, the proposer shall pay insurance premiums in accordance therewith, and the insurer shall assume insurance liability starting from the time agreed thereto.

Article 15   Unless otherwise provided in this Law or in the insurance contract, the proposer may terminate an insurance contract after it has been formed while the insurer may not.

Article 16   When concluding an insurance contract, if the insurer asks questions on the relevant circumstances of the subject matter of insurance or relevant circumstances of the insured, the proposer shall provide truthful information.

If the proposer deliberately, or due to gross negligence, fails to perform its obligation of disclosure as mentioned in the preceding paragraph which failure could influence the insurer on its decision as to whether or not to agree to insure or whether or not to raise the premium rate, the insurer shall have the right to terminate the insurance contract. The right to terminate the contract as specified in the preceding paragraph shall be extinguished if it is not exercised within 30 days after the date on which the insurer learnt of the reason for termination. Once two years have lapsed from the date of formation of the contract, the insurer may not terminate the contract.

If an insured event occurs, the insurer shall bear the obligation of paying indemnities or insurance benefits.

If the proposer deliberately fails to perform its obligation of disclosure, the insurer shall not be liable to pay indemnities or insurance benefits or refund the insurance premiums for insured events that occurred before the termination of the contract.

If the proposer fails to perform its obligation of disclosure due to gross negligence which failure has a material bearing on the occurrence of an insured event, the insurer shall not be liable to pay indemnities or insurance benefits for such insured event if it occurs before the termination of the contract, but shall refund the insurance premiums.

If the insurer, when concluding the contract, was aware that the proposer failed to provide truthful information, it may not terminate the contract.

If an insured event occurs, the insurer shall bear the obligation of paying indemnities or insurance benefits. The term 「insured event」 refers to an event falling within the scope of insurance liability as specified in the insurance contract.

Article 17   If standard clauses provided by the insurer are used when concluding an insurance contract, the application provided to the proposer by the insurer shall have the standard terms attached thereto and the insurer shall explain the provisions of the contract to the proposer.

The insurer shall, when concluding an insurance contract, provide on the application, insurance policy document or other insurance certificate a reminder sufficient to draw the attention of the proposer to the clauses in the insurance contract that exempt it from liability and shall expressly explain the contents of such clauses to the proposer in writing or orally. If no such reminder or express explanation is given, such clauses shall not enter into effect.

Article 18 An insurance contract shall contain the following:

(1) name and domicile of the insurer;

(2) names and domiciles of the proposer and the insured, as well as the name and domicile of the beneficiary in the case of personal insurance;

(3) the subject matter of insurance;

(4) insurance liability and liability exemptions;

(5) term and starting date of coverage;

(6) the insured amount;

(7) insurance premium and the payment method;

(8) method for payment of indemnities or insurance benefits;

(9) liability for breach of contract and dispute resolution;

(10) date of conclusion of contract.

The proposer and the insurer may agree upon other matters relating to the insurance. The term 「beneficiary」 means the person designated by the insured or the proposer in a personal insurance contract with the right to claim the insurance proceeds. The proposer or the insured may be the beneficiary.

The term 「insured amount」 means the maximum amount of indemnities or insurance benefits payable by the insurer.

Article 19 The following terms in an insurance contract concluded using standard clauses provided by the insurer shall be invalid:

(1) terms that exempt the insurer from obligations it is required to bear in accordance with the law or that increase the liability of the proposer or the insured;

(2) terms that deny the rights enjoyed by the proposer, the insured or the beneficiary in accordance with the law.

Article 20 The proposer and the insurer may hold consultations to amend provisions of the contract. Amendment to an insurance contract shall have the insurer endorse the same on the insurance policy document or other insurance certificate or affix an endorsement slip thereto, or have the proposer and the insurer conclude a written agreement on the amendment.

Article 21 The proposer, the insured or the beneficiary shall notify the insurer in a timely manner once they have learnt of the occurrence of an insured event.

If notification is deliberately not given or not given due to gross negligence, making the nature or cause of, or the extent of the losses due to, the insured event difficult to determine, the insurer shall not be liable to pay indemnities or insurance benefits for the portion that is impossible to determine, unless the insurer learnt or ought to have learnt in a timely manner of the occurrence of the insured event by other means.

Article 22 When lodging a claim with the insurer for payment of indemnities or insurance benefits in accordance with the insurance contract after the occurrence of an insured event, the proposer, the insured or the beneficiary shall provide to the insurer all proofs and information it/he/she can provide pertinent to determining the nature or cause of, the extent of the losses due to, and other circumstances of the insured event.

If the insurer, pursuant to the contract, believes that relevant supporting documentation and information is incomplete, it shall, in a timely manner, notify the proposer, the insured or the beneficiary one time to provide the missing documentation or information.

Article 23 Once an insurer receives a claim from the insured or beneficiary for the payment of indemnities or insurance benefits, it shall render its determination in a timely manner.

If the circumstances are complex, it shall render its determination within 30 days, unless otherwise provided in the contract. The insurer shall notify the insured or beneficiary of the results of its determination.

If the claim falls within the insured liability, the insurer shall perform its obligation of paying the indemnities or insurance benefits within 10 days after reaching agreement on paying the indemnities or insurance benefits with the insured or beneficiary.

If the insurance contract provides a time limit for payment of the indemnities or insurance benefits, the insurer shall perform its obligation of paying the indemnities or insurance benefits in accordance with such provisions.

If the insurer fails to perform the obligations listed in the preceding paragraph in a timely manner, in addition to paying the insurance proceeds, it shall also compensate the insured or the beneficiary for losses incurred therefrom. No work unit or individual may unlawfully interfere with the insurer's performance of its obligation to pay indemnities or insurance benefits, nor may it/he/she restrict the rights of the insured or the beneficiary to obtain such payments.

If the age of the insured reported by the proposer is false, resulting in the proposer paying a higher insurance premium than the insurance premium that should have been paid, the insurer shall refund the excess premium to the proposer.

Article 24 After it has rendered its determination pursuant to Article 23 hereof, if the claim does not fall within the insured liability, the insurer shall give written notice to the insured or beneficiary of its refusal to pay indemnities or insurance benefits and give the reasons therefor within three days from the date on which it rendered its determination.

Article 25 If the amount of indemnities or insurance benefits cannot be determined within 60 days after an insurer receives a claim for indemnities or insurance benefits and the relevant proofs and information; the insurer shall first pay the amount that may be determined based on the proofs and information available. After determining the final amount of indemnities or insurance benefits, the insurer shall make up any difference.

Article 26   The period of prescription for the lodging of a claim with the insurer for payment of indemnities or insurance benefits by the insured or beneficiary of an insurance policy other than a life insurance policy shall be two years, counting from the date on which he learnt or ought to have learnt of the occurrence of the insured event.

The period of limitation of actions for the lodging of a claim with the insurer for payment of insurance benefits by the insured or beneficiary of a life insurance policy shall be five years, counting from the date on which he learnt or ought to have learnt of the occurrence of the insured event.

Article 27   If an insured event has not occurred but the insured or beneficiary falsely claims that such an event has occurred, and lodges a claim with the insurer for the payment of indemnities or insurance benefits, the insurer shall have the right to terminate the contract and not return the insurance premiums.

If the proposer or the insured deliberately causes an insured event, the insurer shall have the right to terminate the contract and shall not be liable for the payment of indemnities or insurance benefits. Unless otherwise provided in Article 43 hereof, it will not refund the insurance premiums.

If the proposer, the insured or the beneficiary fabricates false causes for an event or overstates the extent of the losses by means of forged or altered relevant proofs, information or other evidence after the occurrence of such event, the insurer shall not be liable for payment of indemnities or insurance benefits for the portion that is false.

If the proposer, the insured or the beneficiary commits any of the acts specified in the preceding three paragraphs and causes the insurer to pay insurance proceeds or incur expenses, it/he/she shall return the insurance proceeds to or compensate the insurer.

Article 28   「Reinsurance」means that the insurer transfers a portion of its insured business to another insurer in the form of a ceded policy.

At the request of the reinsurer, the reinsurance cedent shall inform the reinsurer in writing of the liability borne by the reinsurance cedent and other circumstances of the original insurance policy.

Article 29   The reinsurer may not request payment of premiums from the proposer of the original insurance policy. The insured or beneficiary of the original insurance policy may not lodge any claim with the reinsurer for payment of indemnities or insurance benefits.

The reinsurance cedent may not refuse to perform or delay the performance of its responsibilities with the original insurance policy on the grounds that the reinsurer has not performed its reinsurance responsibilities.

Article 30 If a dispute arises between an insurer and the proposer, the insured or the beneficiary over the terms of an insurance contract concluded using standard terms provided by the insurer, such terms shall be construed based on the usual understanding thereof. If a contract term permits more than one interpretation, the people's court or arbitration institution shall interpret it in the manner that is favorable to the insured or beneficiary.

Section 2 Personal Insurance Contract

Article 31 A proposer shall have an insurable interest in the following persons:

(1) him/herself;

(2) his/her spouse, children or parents;

(3) other family members or close relatives, in addition to those aforementioned, who have a foster, support or maintenance relationship with the proposer;

(4) employees who have an employment relationship with the proposer.

In addition to the circumstances mentioned in the preceding paragraph, the proposer shall be deemed to have an insurable interest in the insured if the insured consents to the conclusion of the contract by the proposer on his/her behalf. If, at the time of the conclusion of the contract, the proposer does not have an insurable interest in the insured, the contract shall be invalid.

Article 32 If the age of the insured reported by the proposer is false and the insured's true age does not comply with the age restriction specified in the contract, the insurer may terminate the contract and refund, in accordance with the contract, the cash value of the policy. The third paragraph and sixth paragraph of Article 16 hereof shall apply to the exercise by the insurer of its right to terminate the contract.

If the age of the insured reported by the proposer is false, resulting in the proposer paying a lower insurance premium than the insurance premium that should have been paid, the insurer shall have the right to correct the same and request the proposer to make up for the premium in short, or, when paying insurance benefits, disburse the same in proportion to the percentage of the insurance premium that should have been paid accounted for by the insurance premium actually paid.

If the age of the insured reported by the proposer is false, resulting in the proposer paying a higher insurance premium than the insurance premium that should have been paid, the insurer shall refund the excess premium to the proposer

Article 33 A proposer may not take out a personal insurance policy stipulating death as a condition for payment of insurance benefits for a person without capacity for civil acts, and an insurer may not insure the same.

The restrictions of the preceding paragraph shall not apply to personal insurance policies taken out by parents for their minor children. However, the total of the insurance benefits payable upon the death of the insured may not exceed the limit specified by the State Council's insurance regulatory authority.

Article 34 A contract stipulating death as a condition for payment of insurance benefits shall be invalid without the consent of the insured and his/her approval of the insured amount.

An insurance policy document issued in accordance with a contract stipulating death as a condition for payment of insurance benefits may not be transferred or pledged without the written consent of the insured.

The restrictions of the first paragraph hereof shall not apply to personal insurance policies taken out by parents for their minor children.

Article 35 A proposer may, in accordance with the contract, pay the entire insurance premium to the insurer in one lump sum or pay it in installments.

Article 36 If the contract provides for the payment in installments of the insurance premium, and the proposer, after payment of the initial installment of the insurance premium, fails to pay an installment within 30 days after the date of a reminder from the insurer or within 60 days after the specified time limit, the validity of the contract shall be suspended or the insurer shall reduce the insured amount in accordance with the conditions specified in the contract, unless otherwise provided in the contract.

If an insured event occurs in respect of the insured during the period specified in the preceding paragraph, the insurer shall pay the insurance benefits in accordance with the contract, but may deduct the outstanding insurance premium therefrom.

Article 37 If the validity of a contract is suspended in accordance with Article 36 hereof, its validity shall be restored after the insurer and the proposer reach agreement thereon through consultations and the proposer pays the outstanding insurance premium. However, if the parties fail to reach an agreement within two years from the date on which the validity of the contract was suspended, the insurer shall have the right to terminate the contract.

If the insurer terminates the contract pursuant to the preceding paragraph, it shall, in accordance with the contract, refund the cash value of the policy.

Article 38 An insurer may not resort to litigation to require payment from a proposer in respect of life insurance premiums.

Article 39 The beneficiary of a personal insurance policy shall be designated by the insured or proposer. Where the beneficiary is designated by the proposer, the consent of the insured must be obtained.

If a proposer takes out personal insurance policies on workers with whom it/he/she has an employment relationship, it/he/she may not designate anyone other than the insured or their close relatives as beneficiaries.

Where the insured is a person without capacity for civil acts or with limited capacity for civil acts, the beneficiary may be designated by his/her guardian.

Article 40 The insured or proposer may designate one or more persons as beneficiaries. Where there is more than one beneficiary, the order and proportions in which insurance benefits shall be paid shall be determined by the insured or proposer. Where proportions for benefits distribution are not determined, benefits shall be divided equally among the beneficiaries.

Article 41 The insured or proposer may change the beneficiary and shall notify the insurer thereof in writing. Once the insurer receives written notice of the change of beneficiary, it shall endorse the same on the insurance policy document or other insurance certificate or affix an endorsement slip thereto. A change of the beneficiary made by the proposer shall be subject to the consent of the insurer.

Article 42 In any of the following circumstances, if the insured dies, the insurance proceeds shall become part of his/her estate and the insurer shall perform its obligation of paying the insurance benefits in accordance with the PRC Inheritance Law.

(1) no beneficiary was designated or the designation of the beneficiary is unclear and determination thereof is impossible;

(2) the beneficiary dies before the insured, and there is no other beneficiary;

(3) the beneficiary loses or waives his/her beneficiary rights in accordance with the law, and there is no other beneficiary. If the beneficiary and the insured both die in the same event and the sequence of their deaths is impossible to establish, the beneficiary shall be assumed to have died first.

Article 43 If the proposer deliberately causes the death, injury, disability or illness of the insured, the insurer shall not be liable for payment of insurance benefits. Where the proposer has already fully paid insurance premiums for two or more years, the insurer shall refund the cash value of the insurance policy to the other entitled beneficiaries in accordance with the contract.

If a beneficiary deliberately causes the death, injury, disability or illness of the insured or deliberately attempts to murder the insured, such beneficiary shall forfeit his/her beneficiary rights.

Article 44 If a contract stipulates the death of the insured as a condition for payment of insurance benefits and the insured commits suicide within two years from the date of formation of the contract or the restoration of its validity, the insurer shall not be liable to pay the insurance benefits, unless the insured, at the time of his/her suicide, was without civil capacity.

If the insurer is not liable to pay insurance benefits according to the preceding paragraph, it shall, in accordance with the contract, refund the cash value of the policy.

Article 45   If the insured willfully commits a crime or resists lawfully applied criminal enforcement measures, resulting in his/her injury, disability or death, the insurer shall not be liable to pay insurance benefits. If the proposer has paid in full two or more years of insurance premiums, the insurer shall, in accordance with the contract, refund the cash value of the policy.

Article 46   If the occurrence of an insured event such as death, injury, disability or illness of the insured is caused by the act of a third party, the insurer shall not be entitled to the right of recourse against the said third party after paying the insurance benefits to the insured or beneficiary. However, the insured or beneficiary shall still retain the right to claim compensation from the said third party.

Article 47   If the proposer terminates the contract, the insurer shall, in accordance with the contract, refund the cash value of the policy within 30 days from the date of receipt of the notice of termination of the contract.

Section 3   Property Insurance Contract

Article 48   If the insured, at the time of the occurrence of an insured event, does not have an insurable interest in the subject matter of insurance, it/he/she may not lodge a claim with the insurer for payment of indemnities.

Article 49   Where the subject matter of insurance is transferred, the transferee thereof shall succeed to the rights and obligations of the insured.

Where the subject matter of insurance is transferred, the insured or transferee shall notify the insurer in a timely manner, except in the case of cargo insurance contracts and contracts that provide otherwise.

If the transfer of the subject matter of insurance appreciably increases the degree of risk, the insurer may, in accordance with the contract, increase the insurance premium or terminate the contract within 30 days of the date of receipt of the notice specified in the preceding paragraph.

If the insurer terminates the contract, it shall refund to the proposer the insurance premium collected minus, in accordance with the contract, the portion to which it is entitled for the period between the date of commencement of its insurance liability and the date of termination of the contract.

If the insured or the transferee fails to perform its notification obligation as provided in the second paragraph hereof and an insured event occurs due to the appreciable increase in the degree of risk to the subject matter of insurance resulting from the transfer, the insurer shall not be liable to pay indemnities.

Article 50   Cargo insurance contracts or voyage insurance contracts may not be terminated by the contractual parties once the insurance liability has commenced.

Article 51 The insured shall abide by relevant state provisions on fire prevention, safety, production operation, labor protection, etc. in order to protect the safety of the subject matter of insurance. The insurer may, in accordance with the contract, examine the circumstances of the safety of the subject matter of insurance, and issue to the proposer and/or the insured written proposals for the elimination of unsafe factors and hidden dangers.

If either the proposer or insured fails to fulfill its/his/her due diligence requirements towards the safety of the subject matter of insurance in accordance with the contract, the insurer shall have the right to request an increase in the insurance premium or terminate the contract.

Subject to the consent of the insured, the insurer may take precautionary measures to protect the safety of the subject matter of insurance.

Article 52 If the degree of risk to the subject matter of insurance increases appreciably during the term of the contract, the insured shall notify the insurer in accordance with the contract in a timely manner and the insurer may, in accordance with the contract, increase the insurance premium or terminate the contract.

If the insurer terminates the contract, it shall refund to the proposer the insurance premium to commence operations.

If it decides to grant approval, it shall issue a permit to engage in insurance business. If it decides to withhold approval, it shall notify the applicant in writing and give the reasons therefor.

Article 53 In any of the following circumstances, unless the contract has provided otherwise, the insurer shall reduce the insurance premium and refund the appropriate amount of insurance premium calculated on a daily basis:

(1) a change occurs in the circumstances upon which the insurance premium rate was determined, resulting in a marked decrease in the degree of risk to the subject matter of insurance;

(2) the insured value of the subject matter of insurance decreases markedly.

Article 54 If the proposer requests termination of the contract before commencement of the insurance liability, it/he/she shall, in accordance with the contract, pay the service charge to the insurer and the insurer shall refund the insurance premiums.

If the proposer requests termination of the contract after commencement of the insurance liability, the insurer shall refund to the proposer the insurance premiums collected, minus, in accordance with the contract, the portion to which it is entitled for the period between the date of commencement of its insurance liability until the date of termination of the contract.

Article 55 If the proposer and the insurer agree upon the insured value of the subject matter of insurance and specify the same in the contract, the agreed-upon insured value shall serve as the criterion for calculating the indemnities should the subject matter of insurance suffer a loss.

If the proposer and the insurer have not agreed upon the insured value of the subject matter of insurance, the actual value of the subject matter of insurance shall serve as the criterion for calculating the indemnities should the subject matter of insurance suffer a loss.

The insured amount may not exceed the insured value. If the insured amount exceeds the insured value, the portion exceeding the insured value shall be invalid and the insurer shall refund the corresponding portion of the insurance premiums.

If the insured amount is less than the insured value, the insurer shall, unless otherwise specified in the contract, be liable for payment of the indemnities in proportion to the percentage of the insured value accounted for by the insured amount.

Article 56 Information relevant to overlapping insurance shall be reported by the proposer to all concerned insurers.

The total of indemnities payable by the insurers in the event of overlapping insurance may not exceed the insured value. Unless otherwise specified in the contracts, each insurer shall be liable for payment of the indemnities in proportion to the percentage of the total insured amount accounted for by its insured amount.

The proposer of overlapping insurance may, in respect of the portion of the total insured amount exceeding the insured value, request that each insurer refund the insurance premiums pro rata.

The term「overlapping insurance」means insurance where the proposer concludes insurance contracts with two or more insurers in respect of the same subject matter of insurance, the same insurable interest and the same insured events, and the total of the insured amounts exceeds the insured value.

Article 57 When an insured event occurs, the insured shall, with due diligence, take necessary measures to prevent or mitigate losses.

The necessary and reasonable expenses incurred by the insured in the prevention or mitigation of losses of the subject matter of insurance after the occurrence of an insured event shall be borne by the insurer. The amount of such expenses shall be calculated separately from the amount of compensation for the losses of the subject matter of insurance, and the maximum shall not exceed the insured amount.

Article 58 If part of the subject matter of insurance suffers a loss, the proposer may terminate the contract within 30 days of compensation from the insurer; and, unless otherwise provided by the contract, the insurer may also terminate the contract but shall notify the proposer 15 days in advance.

If the contract is terminated, the insurer shall refund to the proposer the insurance premiums for the portion of the subject matter of insurance that did not suffer a loss, minus, in accordance with the contract, the portion to which it is entitled for the period between the date of commencement of its insurance liability until the date of termination of the contract.

Article 59 After the occurrence of an insured event, where the insurer has paid the insured amount in full and the insured amount is the same as the insured value, all rights to the damaged subject matter of insurance shall pass to the insurer, or, where the insured amount is less than the insured value, the insurer shall obtain partial rights to the damaged subject matter of insurance in proportion to the percentage of the insured value accounted for by the insured amount.

Article 60 Where an insured event occurs due to damage to the subject matter of insurance caused by a third party, the insurer may, from the date of payment of indemnities to the insured, exercise the insured's right to claim compensation from the third party by subrogation within the amount of indemnities.

Where the insured has already obtained damages from the third party following the occurrence of an insured event mentioned in the preceding paragraph, the insurer may, when paying the indemnities, appropriately deduct the amount of compensation obtained by the insured from the third party.

The exercise by the insurer of its right to claim compensation by subrogation in accordance with the first paragraph hereof shall not affect the insured's right to claim compensation from the third party for the portion that has not been compensated.

Article 61 Where the insured waives its right to claim compensation from the third party after the occurrence of an insured event and before the insurer pays indemnities, the insurer shall not be liable for the payment of indemnities.

If after the insurer has paid indemnities to the insured, the insured, without the consent of the insurer, waives its/his/her right to claim compensation from the third party, such waiver shall be deemed invalid.

If due to a deliberate act or gross negligence by the insured, the insurer cannot exercise its right to claim compensation by subrogation, it may deduct, or demand reimbursement of, the corresponding portion of the indemnities.

Article 62 Except where the family members or members of the household of the insured deliberately cause an insured event specified in the first paragraph of Article 60 hereof, the insurer may not exercise the right to claim compensation by subrogation from family members or members of the household of the insured.

Article 63 When the insurer exercises its right to claim compensation from a third party by subrogation, the insured shall provide the insurer the necessary documents and relevant circumstances it/he/she has learnt.

Article 64　The necessary and reasonable expenses incurred by the insurer and the insured in the investigation and determination of the nature or cause of an insured event and the extent of the losses incurred by the subject matter of insurance shall be borne by the insurer.

Article 65　For damage to a third party caused by the insured of a liability insurance policy, the insurer may directly pay indemnities to the third party in accordance with the law or the contract.

If the insured of a liability insurance policy causes damage to a third party and the compensation liability owed to the third party by the insured have been determined, the insurer shall, at the request of the insured, pay the indemnities directly to the third party.

If the insured fails to make such request, the third party shall have the right to directly lodge a claim with the insurer for payment of indemnities in respect of the portion of the compensation he/she is owed.

If the insured of a liability insurance policy causes damage to a third party and fails to compensate the third party, the insurer may not pay indemnities to the insured.

The term「liability insurance」means insurance of which the subject matter is the liability borne by the insured to compensate a third party in accordance with the law.

Article 66　If arbitration or litigation proceedings are instituted against the insured of a liability insurance policy due to an insured event that caused damage to a third party, the arbitration or litigation costs and other necessary and reasonable expenses paid by the insured shall be borne by the insurer, unless otherwise provided by the contract.

Chapter Ⅲ　Insurance Companies

Article 67　Establishment of insurance companies shall be subject to the approval of the State Council's insurance regulatory authority.

When examining the application for the establishment of an insurance company, the State Council's insurance regulatory authority shall take into consideration the development of the insurance industry and the requirements of fair competition.

Article 68　The following conditions shall be met for the establishment of an insurance company:

(1) the main shareholders having the capacity for sustained profitability, a good reputation, not having a record of a major violation of laws or regulations during the most recent three years and having net assets of not less than RMB 200 million;

(2) having articles of association in compliance with this Law and the PRC Company Law;

(3) having the registered capital as specified herein;

(4) having directors, supervisors and senior management personnel with the professional knowledge of their positions and work experience in the business;

(5) having a sound organizational structure and management system;

(6) having a place of business that meets the requirements, and having other business-related facilities;

(7) other conditions as specified by laws, administrative regulations or the State Council's insurance regulatory authority.

Article 69　The minimum registered capital required for the establishment of an insurance company shall be RMB 200 million.

The State Council's insurance regulatory authority may, based on the scope of business and the size of insurance companies, adjust the minimum registered capital provided that the same is not lower than the limit specified in the first paragraph hereof.

The registered capital of an insurance company must be paid-in monetary capital.

Article 70　When applying to establish an insurance company, a written application and the following materials shall be submitted to the State Council's insurance regulatory authority:

(1) an application letter for establishment, specifying the name, registered capital and scope of business, etc. of the proposed insurance company;

(2) a feasibility study report;

(3) a plan for the preparation for establishment;

(4) the business licenses or other background information of the investors and their financial accounting reports for the previous year audited by an accounting firm;

(5) a list containing the names of the person in charge of the preparatory committee and the proposed chairman of the board and managers approved by the investors and those person's proofs of acceptance;

(6) other materials as specified by the State Council's insurance regulatory authority.

Article 71　The State Council's insurance regulatory authority shall examine the application for the establishment of an insurance company, render its decision on whether or not to grant approval for preparation of establishment and notify the applicant thereof in writing within six months from the date of acceptance of the application. If it decides to withhold approval, it shall give the reasons therefor in writing.

Article 72　The applicant shall complete the preparatory work within one year from the date of receipt of the notice of approval for preparation of establishment. It may not engage in insurance business activities during the preparatory period.

Article 73　If the applicant meets the conditions for establishment set forth in Article 68 hereof after completion of the preparatory work, it may submit to the State Council's regulatory authority an application to commence operations.

The State Council's insurance regulatory authority shall render its decision on whether or not to grant approval for commencement of operations within 60 days from the date of acceptance of the application to commence operations.

If it decides to grant approval, it shall issue a permit to engage in insurance business. If it decides to withhold approval, it shall notify the applicant in writing and give the reasons therefor.

Article 74 An insurance company shall obtain approval of the insurance regulatory authority for establishment of a (sub-) branch in the People's Republic of China.

The (sub-) branch of an insurance company shall have no legal personality and its civil liability shall be borne by the insurance company.

Article 75 When an insurance company wishes to establish a (sub-) branch, it shall submit a written application and the following materials to the insurance regulatory authority:

(1) a written application for establishment;

(2) a three-year business development plan for the proposed institution and market analysis materials;

(3) the resumes of the proposed senior management personnel and relevant supporting documentation;

(4) other materials as specified by the State Council's insurance regulatory authority.

Article 76 The insurance regulatory authority shall examine the application for the establishment of a (sub-) branch of an insurance company and render its decision on whether or not to grant approval within 60 days from the date of acceptance of the application. If it decides to grant approval, it shall issue a permit for the (sub-) branch to engage in insurance business. If it decides to withhold approval, it shall notify the applicant in writing and give the reason therefor.

Article 77 An insurance company or a (sub-) branch thereof that has been granted approval for establishment shall carry out registration procedures with, and collect its business license from, the administration for industry and commerce on the strength of its permit to engage in insurance business.

Article 78 If an insurance company or a (sub-) branch thereof fails to register with the administration for industry and commerce within six months from the date on which it obtained its permit to engage in insurance business without a legitimate reason, its permit to engage in insurance business shall become null and void.

Article 79 An insurance company shall obtain the approval of the State Council's insurance regulatory authority for establishment of a subsidiary, (sub-) branch or representative office outside the People's Republic of China.

Article 80 If a foreign insurance institution wishes to establish a representative office in the People's Republic of China, it shall require the approval of the State Council's insurance regulatory authority. Such representative office may not engage in insurance business activities.

Article 81　The directors, supervisors and senior management personnel of an insurance company shall be of good conduct, be familiar with insurance-related laws and administrative regulations, have the operations and management capabilities required to perform their duties and have obtained, before taking up their positions, approval of their qualifications for their positions from the insurance regulatory authority.

The scope of the senior management personnel of insurance companies shall be specified by the State Council's insurance regulatory authority.

Article 82　If any of the circumstances set forth in Article 147 of the PRC Company Law or set forth below applies to a person, he/she may not serve as a director, supervisor or member of the senior management personnel of an insurance company:

(1) he/she was a director, supervisor or member of the senior management personnel of a financial institution who had his or her qualifications for the position revoked by the financial regulator due to a violation of the law or a breach of discipline and less than five years have lapsed since the date of such revocation;

(2) he/she was a lawyer, chartered accountant or a professional in an asset appraisal firm, verification firm or other such firm who had his or her practice qualifications revoked due to a violation of the law or a breach of discipline and less than five years have lapsed since the date of such revocation.

Article 83　If a director, supervisor or member of the senior management personnel of an insurance company violates laws or administrative regulation or breaches the company's articles of association in the course of performing his or her company duties, thereby causing the company to incur a loss, he/she shall be liable for compensation.

Article 84　An insurance company shall obtain approval from the insurance regulatory authority for any of the following circumstances:

(1) change of name;

(2) change of registered capital;

(3) change of the place of business of the company or of any (sub-) branch;

(4) cancellation of a (sub-) branch;

(5) division or merger of the company;

(6) amendment to the company's articles of association;

(7) a change in a shareholder whose capital contribution accounts for at least 5% of the total capital of the limited liability company or in a shareholder who holds at least 5% of the shares of the company limited by shares;

(8) another circumstance as specified by the State Council's insurance regulatory author-

ity.

Article 85　An insurance company shall employ actuarial professionals certified by the State Council's insurance regulatory authority, and shall establish systems for actuarial reporting.

An insurance company shall engage professionals and establish a compliance reporting system.

Article 86　An insurance company shall submit relevant reports, statements, documents and information in accordance with the provisions of the insurance regulatory authority.

The solvency reports, financial accounting reports, actuarial reports, compliance reports and other relevant reports, statements, documents and information of an insurance company shall truthfully record insurance business matters and may not contain false records, misleading statements or material omissions.

Article 87　An insurance company shall duly keep complete account books, original vouchers and relevant information pertaining to its business activities in accordance with the provisions of the State Council's insurance regulatory authority.

The period for keeping the account books, original vouchers and relevant information mentioned in the preceding paragraph shall be counted from the date on which the insurance contract ends and shall be not less than five years for an insurance term of less than one year and not less than 10 years for an insurance term of more than one year.

Article 88　When an insurance company intends to engage or dismiss an accounting firm, asset appraisal firm, credit rating agency or other such intermediary firm, it shall report the same to the insurance regulatory authority. If it intends to dismiss its accounting firm, asset appraisal firm, credit rating agency or other such intermediary firm, it shall give the reason therefor.

Article 89　If an insurance company needs to be dissolved as a result of a division or merger, or if the shareholders' meeting or shareholders' general meeting resolves to dissolve it, or if a reason for dissolution as specified in the company's articles of association arises, it shall be dissolved following the approval of the State Council's insurance regulatory authority.

An insurance company engaging in life insurance business may not be dissolved for any reason other than division, merger or its being closed down in accordance with the law.

When an insurance company is dissolved, a liquidation committee shall be established in accordance with the law to liquidate it.

Article 90　If the circumstances specified in Article 2 of the PRC Enterprise Bankruptcy Law apply to an insurance company, the insurance company or its creditors may, with the consent of the State Council's insurance regulatory authority, apply to a people's court in accordance with the law for restructuring, settlement or bankruptcy liquidation. The State Council's insurance regulatory authority may also apply to the people's court in accordance with the law for the restructuring or bankruptcy liquidation of said insurance company.

Article 91 After the discharge on a priority basis of the bankruptcy expenses and debts of common interest, the property in bankruptcy shall be applied in the following sequence:

(1) payment of the outstanding wages, medical subsidies, disability subsidies and disability and death pensions of employees, outstanding basic old-age insurance and basic medical insurance premiums payable into employees' personal accounts and compensation payable to employees as specified in laws and administrative regulations;

(2) payment of indemnities or insurance benefits;

(3) payment of the insurance company's outstanding social insurance premiums, other than those specified in Item (1), and outstanding taxes;

(4) payment of ordinary bankruptcy claims investigation notice, the work unit or individual being inspected or investigated shall have the right to refuse such monitoring inspection or investigation.

If the property in bankruptcy is insufficient to discharge all of the claims at one level of the sequence, it shall be distributed pro rata.

The wages of the directors, supervisors and senior management personnel of a bankrupt insurance company shall be calculated at the average wage of the company's employees.

Article 92 If an insurance company that engages in life insurance business is closed down in accordance with the law or is declared bankrupt in accordance with the law, its life insurance contracts and liability reserve must be transferred to another insurance company that engages in life insurance business.

If it fails to reach a transfer agreement with another insurance company, the State Council's insurance regulatory authority shall designate an insurance company that engages in life insurance business to accept the transfer.

The transfer or the designated acceptance of the transfer by the State Council's insurance regulatory authority of the life insurance contracts and liability reserve as specified in the preceding paragraph shall safeguard the lawful rights and interests of the insured and beneficiaries.

Article 93 If an insurance company terminates its business operations in accordance with the law, its permit to engage in insurance business shall be cancelled.

Article 94 Unless otherwise provided herein, the PRC Company Law shall apply to insurance companies.

Chapter Ⅳ Insurance Business Rules

Article 95 The scope of business of insurance companies shall include:

(1) personal insurance business, including insurance business such as life insurance, health insurance and accidental injury insurance;

(2) property insurance business, including insurance business such as property loss insurance, liability insurance, credit insurance and guarantee insurance;

(3) other business related to insurance as approved by the State Council's insurance regulatory authority.

An insurer may not concurrently engage in personal insurance business and property insurance business. However, an insurance company engaging in property insurance business may, with the approval of the State Council's insurance regulatory authority, engage in short-term health insurance business and accidental injury insurance business.

An insurance company shall engage in insurance business activities within its scope of business approved by the State Council's insurance regulatory authority in accordance with the law.

Article 96 Subject to the approval of the State Council's insurance regulatory authority, insurance companies may engage in the following reinsurance business for insurance business specified in Article 95 hereof:

(1) ceding reinsurance;

(2) assuming reinsurance.

Article 97 An insurance company shall allocate 20% of its total registered capital as a security bond and deposit the same with a bank designated by the State Council's insurance regulatory authority. Such security bond may not be used except to discharge debts when the company is liquidated.

Article 98 Insurance companies shall make allocations to various liability reserves based on the principle of protecting the interests of the insured and guaranteeing solvency. Specific measures for the allocation and carry-over of funds to liability reserves by insurance companies shall be formulated by the State Council's insurance regulatory authority.

Article 99 An insurance company shall make allocations to a common reserve fund.

Article 100 An insurance company shall make contributions to an insurance security fund. Such insurance security fund shall be managed centrally and use thereof shall be made in a coordinated manner in the following circumstances:

(1) to provide relief to proposers, insured and beneficiaries when an insurance company is closed down or is declared bankrupt;

(2) to provide relief to the insurance company that accepts in accordance with the law its life insurance contracts when an insurance company is closed down or is declared bankrupt;

(3) other circumstances as specified by the State Council. The specific measures for the funding, management and use of the insurance security fund shall be formulated by the State

Council.

The specific measures for the funding, management and use of the insurance security fund shall be formulated by the State Council.

Article 101 An insurance company shall have the minimum solvency appropriate to the size of its business and its degree of risk. The difference derived by subtracting an insurance company's admissible liabilities from its admissible assets may not be lower than the figure specified by the State Council's insurance regulatory authority. If such difference falls below the specified figure, the insurance company shall, as required by the State Council's insurance regulatory authority, take appropriate measures to reach such figure.

Article 102 The self-retained insurance premiums of a year of an insurance company engaging in property insurance business may not exceed four times the sum of its paid-in capital and common reserve.

Article 103 The liability borne by an insurance company for each risk unit, that is, the maximum range of loss that may be caused by a single insured event, may not be more than 10% of the sum of its paid-in capital and common reserve. The portion exceeding the sum shall be reinsured.

The demarcation of risk units by an insurance company shall comply with the provisions of the State Council's insurance regulatory authority.

Article 104 An insurance company's methodology for demarcating risk units and its arrangement for catastrophic risks shall be submitted to the State Council's insurance regulatory authority for the record.

Article 105 An insurance company shall arrange for reinsurance in accordance with the provisions of the State Council's insurance regulatory authority, and prudently select the reinsurer.

Article 106 An insurance company shall apply its capital in a sound manner and comply with the principle of safety. The application of an insurance company's capital shall be limited to the following:

(1) bank deposits;

(2) purchase and sale of negotiable securities, such as bonds, stocks and securities investment fund shares;

(3) investment in immovable property;

(4) other means of capital application as specified by the State Council. The specific measures for the administration of the application of insurance company capital shall be formulated by the State Council's insurance regulatory authority based on the preceding two paragraphs.

The specific measures for the administration of the application of insurance company capital shall be formulated by the State Council's insurance regulatory authority based on the preceding two paragraphs.

Article 107   With the approval of the State Council's insurance regulatory authority in concert with the State Council's securities regulatory authority, an insurance company may establish an insurance asset management company.

In engaging in securities investment activities, an insurance asset management company shall comply with laws and administrative regulations such as the PRC Securities Law.

The measures for the administration of insurance asset management companies shall be formulated by the State Council's insurance regulatory authority in concert with relevant State Council departments.

Article 108   An insurance company shall establish a system for the management of, and disclosure of information on, affiliated transactions in accordance with the provisions of the State Council's insurance regulatory authority.

Article 109   The controlling shareholder (s), de facto controller (s), directors, supervisors and senior management personnel of an insurance company may not use affiliated transactions to harm the interests of the company.

Article 110   An insurance company shall truthfully, accurately and completely disclose its financial accounting reports, risk management position, details of its insurance product business and other such material matters in accordance with the provisions of the State Council's insurance regulatory authority.

Article 111   An insurance company's insurance salespersons shall satisfy the qualification conditions specified by the State Council's insurance regulatory authority and have a qualification certificate issued by the insurance regulatory authority.

The scope, and the measures for the administration of, the insurance salespersons mentioned in the preceding paragraph shall be specified by the State Council's insurance regulatory authority.

Article 112   An insurance company shall establish a system for the registration and management of insurance agents, enhance the training and management of insurance agents and may not incite or induce insurance agents to engage in activities that breach their obligation of good faith.

Article 113   An insurance company and its (sub-) branches shall use their permits to engage in insurance business in accordance with the law and may not transfer, lease out or lend out such permits.

Article 114   An insurance company shall draft its insurance terms and premium rates in a fair and reasonable manner in accordance with the provisions of the State Council's insurance regulatory authority and may not harm the lawful rights and interests of proposers, insured and beneficiaries.

An insurance company shall perform its obligation of paying indemnities or insurance benefits in accordance with its contracts and this Law in a timely manner.

Article 115 In engaging in its business, an insurance company shall comply with the principle of fair competition and may not engage in unfair competition.

Article 116 Insurance companies and their working personnel may not commit any of the following acts in the course of insurance business activities:

(1) defrauding the proposer, insured or beneficiary;

(2) concealing important circumstances pertinent to the insurance contract from the proposer;

(3) hindering the proposer from performing, or inducing the proposer not to perform, its/his/her obligation of disclosure as specified herein;

(4) offering or promising to offer rebates on insurance premiums or other benefits not specified in the insurance contract to the proposer, insured, or beneficiary;

(5) refusing to perform, in accordance with the law, the obligation to pay insurance indemnities or benefits as specified in the insurance contract;

(6) deliberately fabricating insured events or insurance contracts or overstating the extent of losses incurred by an insured event that has happened to lodge falsified claims, fraudulently obtain insurance proceeds or obtain other improper gains;

(7) diverting, retaining or misappropriating insurance premiums;

(8) engaging, for the purpose of conducting insurance sales activities, an organization or individual that lacks lawful qualifications;

(9) exploiting its/his/her engagement in the insurance business to seek improper gains for another organization or individual;

(10) using an insurance agent, insurance brokerage or insurance assessor to engage in illegal activities such as illicitly obtaining fees by engaging in fictitious insurance intermediary business or fabricating cancellation of insurance policies, etc.;

(11) damaging the goodwill of a competitor through means such as the fabrication and dissemination of false facts, or engaging in other acts of unfair competition to disturb the order of the insurance market;

(12) divulging the trade secrets of proposers or insured learnt in the course of business activities;

(13) committing other acts that violate laws, administrative regulations or provisions of the State Council's insurance regulatory authority.

Chapter Ⅴ Insurance Agents And Insurance Brokerages

Article 117 Insurance agents shall be institutions or individuals engaged by an insurer to handle insurance business on behalf of the insurer within the scope of the insurer's authorization and that charge a commission fee from the insurer.

Insurance agencies include both dedicated insurance agencies that engage exclusively in insurance agency business and non-dedicated insurance agencies that engage in insurance agency business as a sideline.

Article 118 An insurance brokerage is an institution that, based upon the interests of the proposer, provides intermediary services for the conclusion of an insurance contract between the proposer and insurer, and that charges a commission fee in accordance with the law.

Article 119 An insurance agency or brokerage shall possess the qualifications specified by the State Council's insurance regulatory authority, or obtain a permit to engage in insurance agency business or an insurance brokerage business license issued by the insurance regulatory authority.

A dedicated insurance agency or an insurance brokerage shall carry out registration procedures with, and collect its business license from, the administration for industry and commerce on the strength of its permit issued by the insurance regulatory authority.

A non-dedicated insurance agency shall carry out amendment of registration procedures with the administration for industry and commerce on the strength of its permit issued by the insurance regulatory authority.

Article 120 The provisions of the PRC Company Law on minimum registered capital shall apply to a dedicated insurance agency or an insurance brokerage established in the form of a company.

The State Council's insurance regulatory authority may, based on the scope of business and size of dedicated insurance agencies and insurance brokerages, adjust their minimum registered capital provided that the same is not lower than the limit specified in the PRC Company Law.

The registered capital of, or capital contributions to, a dedicated insurance agency or an insurance brokerage must be paid-in monetary capital.

Article 121 The senior management personnel of a dedicated insurance agency or an insurance brokerage shall be of good conduct, be familiar with insurance laws and administrative regulations, have the operation and management capabilities required to perform their duties and have obtained, before taking up their positions, approval of their qualifications for their positions from the insurance regulatory authority.

Article 122 Individual insurance agents, practicing personnel of insurance agencies and practicing personnel of insurance brokerages shall satisfy the qualification conditions specified by the State Council's insurance regulatory authority and have a qualification certificate issued by the insurance regulatory authority.

Article 123 Insurance agencies and insurance brokerages shall have their own places of business and keep dedicated account books for recording the receipts and expenditures relating to insurance agency or brokerage business.

Article 124 An insurance agency or insurance brokerage shall deposit a security bond or take out professional liability insurance in accordance with the provisions of the State Council's insurance regulatory authority. An insurance agency or insurance brokerage may not use its security bond without the approval of the insurance regulatory authority.

Article 125 An individual insurance agent may not concurrently accept appointment from more than one insurer when handling life insurance business on an agency basis.

Article 126 When engaging an insurance agent to handle insurance business on its behalf, an insurer shall conclude an agency agreement with the insurance agent specifying, in accordance with the law, the rights and obligations of both parties.

Article 127 An insurer shall bear the liability for acts of an insurance agent when handling insurance business on behalf of the insurer in accordance with the insurer's authorization.

If an insurance agent, in the absence of authorization, or by exceeding its authorization or after the termination of its authorization, enters into a contract in the name of the insurer, thereby giving the proposer reason to believe that its has such authorization, such agency act shall be valid. The insurer may pursue, in accordance with the law, liability of the insurance agent that acted ultra vires.

Article 128 If an insurance brokerage causes a proposer or the insured to incur a loss due to negligence, it shall be liable for compensation.

Article 129 The parties to an insurance activity may engage an insurance assessor or other such lawfully established independent assessor or a person with the relevant professional knowledge to appraise and assess an insured event.

The organization or individual engaged to appraise or assess the insured event shall do so in a lawful, independent, objective and impartial manner, and no work unit or individual may interfere in such appraisal or assessment.

If the organization or individual mentioned in the preceding paragraph causes the insurer or the insured to incur a loss due to a deliberate act or negligence, it/he/she shall be liable for compensation in accordance with the law.

Article 130 Insurance commission fees shall be paid only to lawfully qualified insurance agents or brokerages, and may not be paid to any other parties.

Article 131　An insurance agent, or insurance brokerage or its practicing personnel may not commit any of the following acts in the course of its or their business activities:

(1) defrauding the insurer, proposer, insured or beneficiary;

(2) concealing important circumstances pertinent to the insurance contract;

(3) hindering the proposer from performing, or inducing the proposer not to perform, its/his/her obligation of disclosure as specified herein;

(4) offering or promising to offer other benefits not specified in the insurance contract to the proposer, insured or beneficiary;

(5) exploiting administrative power, position or occupational advantages, or using other improper means to force a proposer to conclude an insurance contract, or entice it/him/her into or restrict it/him/her from concluding such contract;

(6) forging an insurance contract or amending the same without authorization, or providing fraudulent supporting documentation for the parties to the contract;

(7) diverting, retaining or misappropriating insurance premiums or insurance proceeds;

(8) exploiting business advantages to seek illegitimate gains for another organization or individual;

(9) colluding with a proposer, the insured or the beneficiary to obtain insurance proceeds by fraud;

(10) divulging the trade secrets of the insurer, proposers or insured learnt in the course of business activities.

Article 132　The division, merger or change in organizational form of, the establishment of a (sub-) branch by, and the dissolution of, a dedicated insurance agency or an insurance brokerage shall be subject to the approval of the insurance regulatory authority.

Article 133　The first paragraph of Article 86 and Article 113 hereof shall apply to insurance agencies and brokerages.

Chapter Ⅵ　Oversight Of The Insurance Industry

Article 134　An insurance regulatory authority shall oversee the insurance industry, safeguard the order of the insurance market and protect the lawful rights and interests of proposers, insured and beneficiaries in accordance with this Law, within the purview specified by the State Council and in compliance with the principles of lawfulness, transparency and impartiality.

Article 135　The State Council's insurance regulatory authority shall formulate and issue rules on the oversight of the insurance industry in accordance with laws and administrative regulations.

Article 136 Insurance terms and insurance premium rates for types of insurance that are of an immediate interest to the public, types of insurance that are mandatory in accordance with the law and newly-developed types of life insurance shall be submitted to the State Council's insurance regulatory authority for approval.

When conducting its examination and granting its approval, the State Council's insurance regulatory authority shall comply with the principles of protecting the public interest and guarding against unfair competition. The insurance terms and insurance premium rates for other types of insurance shall be submitted to the insurance regulatory authority for the record.

The specific measures for the examination, approval and record filing of insurance terms and insurance premium rates shall be formulated by the State Council's insurance regulatory authority based on the preceding paragraph.

Article 137 If the insurance terms or insurance premium rates used by an insurance company violate laws, administrative regulations or relevant provisions of the State Council's insurance regulatory authority, the insurance regulatory authority shall order the insurance company to cease using the same or revise the same within a specified period of time.

If the circumstances are serious, it may ban the insurance company from filing new insurance terms and premium rates for a certain period of time.

Article 138 The State Council's insurance regulatory authority shall establish a sound system for regulation of the solvency of insurance companies to monitor the solvency of insurance companies.

Article 139 If an insurance company has inadequate solvency, the State Council's insurance regulatory authority shall place it on a watch list and may, depending on the specific circumstances, take the following measures:

(1) order it to increase its capital, or arrange for reinsurance;

(2) restrict its scope of business;

(3) restrict its distribution of dividends to shareholders;

(4) restrict its purchase of fixed assets or place restrictions on the scale of its operating expenses;

(5) restrict the manner in which it applies its capital and the percentage thereof;

(6) restrict its establishment of additional (sub-) branches;

(7) order it to auction bad assets and/or transfer insurance business;

(8) place restrictions on the salary level of its directors, supervisors and senior management personnel;

(9) place restrictions on its commercial advertising;

(10) order it to cease accepting new business.

Article 140 If an insurance company fails to allocate or carry over funds to its various liability reserves in accordance herewith, or to arrange for reinsurance in accordance herewith, or seriously violates the provisions hereof on the application of capital, the insurance regulatory authority shall order it to correct the matter within a specified period of time and may order it to replace the person in charge and relevant management personnel.

Article 141 If after the insurance regulatory authority has, in accordance with Article 140 hereof, rendered a decision on correction within a specified period of time, the insurance company does not do so within the specified period of time, the State Council's insurance regulatory authority may make a decision to select and appoint insurance professionals and designate relevant personnel of the insurance company to form a rectification team to carry out rectification of the company.

The rectification decision shall state the name of the company under rectification, cause for rectification, members of the rectification team and the time limit for the rectification, and shall be announced.

Article 142 The rectification team shall have the right to oversee the day-to-day business of the insurance company undergoing rectification. The person in charge and the relevant management personnel of the company undergoing rectification shall exercise their functions and powers under the supervision of the rectification team.

Article 143 An insurance company undergoing rectification shall continue to engage in its existing business during the rectification period. However, the State Council's insurance regulatory authority may order the company undergoing rectification to cease engaging in a part of its existing business or to cease accepting new business and make revisions to the application of its capital.

Article 144 If an insurance company undergoing rectification, following the rectification, has remedied its violation hereof and resumed its normal operations, the rectification team shall submit a report, the rectification shall conclude once the State Council's insurance regulatory authority gives its approval, and the State Council's insurance regulatory authority shall make an announcement to that effect.

Article 145 The State Council's insurance regulatory authority may take over an insurance company if:

(1) the company's solvency is seriously deficient;

(2) the company violates this Law and such violation harms the public interest and could or has seriously jeopardized the company's solvency. The claims relationships and debts relationships of an insurance company that has been taken over shall not change as a result of the takeover.

Article 146 The constitution of the takeover team and implementing measures for the takeover shall be decided by the State Council's insurance regulatory authority and shall be announced.

Article 147　The State Council's insurance regulatory authority may make a decision to extend the takeover period upon its expiration; however the maximum takeover period may not exceed two years.

Article 148　If the insurance company being taken over has been restored to its normal capacity for operations at the expiration of the takeover period, the State Council's insurance regulatory authority shall make a decision to terminate the takeover and announce the same.

Article 149　If the circumstances specified in Article 2 of the PRC Enterprise Bankruptcy Law apply to an insurance company that is undergoing rectification or that has been taken over, the State Council's insurance regulatory authority may apply to a people's court in accordance with the law for the restructuring or bankruptcy liquidation of said insurance company.

Article 150　If an insurance company has its permit to engage in insurance business revoked as a result of illegal operations or if its solvency is inferior to the standard set by the State Council's insurance regulatory authority and not closing down such company would seriously jeopardise the order of the insurance market and/or harm the public interest, the State Council's insurance regulatory authority shall close it down, announce the same and constitute a liquidation committee in a timely manner in accordance with the law to liquidate it.

Article 151　The State Council's insurance regulatory authority shall have the right to demand that the shareholders and de facto controller(s) of an insurance company provide relevant information and data within a specified period of time.

Article 152　If a shareholder of an insurance company uses affiliated transactions to seriously harm the company's interests, jeopardizing its solvency, the State Council's insurance regulatory authority shall order it to rectify the matter. Until it effects rectification as required, the State Council's insurance regulatory authority may place restrictions on its shareholder rights. If the shareholder refuses to rectify the matter, the State Council's insurance regulatory authority may order it to transfer the equity it holds in the insurance company.

Article 153　As required to perform its oversight duties, an insurance regulatory authority may have a regulatory discussion with the directors, supervisors and senior management personnel of an insurance company and ask them to provide an explanation of material matters of the company's business activities and risk management.

Article 154　When an insurance company is undergoing rectification, has been taken over or is undergoing liquidation after being closed down or when a material risk arises, the State Council's insurance regulatory authority may take the following measures against the directors, supervisors and senior management personnel who are directly in charge of the company and other directly responsible persons:

1. notify the exit control authorities to prevent, in accordance with the law, them leaving the country; and

2. apply to the judicial authorities to prohibit them from removing elsewhere, transferring or otherwise disposing of property, or encumbering other rights to property.

Article 155 In performing its duties in accordance with the law, an insurance regulatory authority may take the following measures:

(1) conduct onsite inspections of insurance companies, insurance agencies, insurance brokerages, insurance asset management companies and representative offices of foreign insurance institutions;

(2) enter premises where a violation of the law is suspected of having occurred to investigate and gather evidence;

(3) question concerned parties, and questioning work units and individuals that have a connection with the event being investigated and require them to give an explanation of matters relating to the event being investigated;

(4) review and take copies of information such as property title registrations that have a connection with the event being investigated;

(5) review and take copies of the financial accounting information and other relevant documents and information of insurance companies, insurance agencies, insurance brokerages, insurance asset management companies and representative offices of foreign insurance institutions and of work units and individuals that have a connection with the event being investigated, seal documents and information that could be removed elsewhere, concealed or destroyed;

(6) check the bank accounts of insurance companies, insurance agencies, insurance brokerages, insurance asset management companies and representative offices of foreign insurance institutions that are suspected of having operated in violation of the law and work units and individuals that have a connection with the suspected violation of the law;

(7) where there is evidence that implicated property, such as unlawful funds, has been or could be removed elsewhere or concealed, or there is evidence that important evidence has been or could be concealed, fabricated or destroyed, subject to the approval of the person in charge of the insurance regulatory authority, apply to a people's court for the freezing or placement under seal thereof. If an insurance regulatory authority is to take the measures set forth in Item (1), (2) or (5) of the preceding paragraph, it shall require the approval of the person in charge of the insurance regulatory authority. If it is to take the measure set forth in Item (6), it shall require the approval of the person in charge of the State Council's insurance regulatory authority.

When an insurance regulatory authority is conducting a monitoring inspection or investigation in accordance with the law, its inspectors or investigators may not be fewer than two and they shall present their credentials and the monitoring inspection or investigation notice.

If there are fewer than two inspectors or investigators or if they fail to present their credentials and the monitoring inspection or investigation notice, the work unit or individual being inspected or investigated shall have the right to refuse such monitoring inspection or investigation.

Article 156 When an insurance regulatory authority is carrying out its duties in accordance with the law, the work unit or individual being inspected or investigated shall co-operate therewith.

Article 157 The members of the working personnel of an insurance regulatory authority shall be devoted to their duties, handle matters in accordance with the law, be impartial, be of high integrity, may not use the advantages of their positions to seek improper gains and may not divulge the trade secrets of relevant work units and individuals to which they have been privy.

Article 158 The State Council's insurance regulatory authority shall establish with the People's Bank of China and other financial regulatory authorities of the State Council a mechanism for the sharing of regulatory information. When an insurance regulatory authority is carrying out its duties in accordance with the law by conducting a monitoring inspection or investigation, relevant departments shall co-operate therewith.

Chapter VII Legal Liability

Article 159 If this Law is violated by establishing an insurance company or insurance asset management company without authorisation, or by unlawfully engaging in commercial insurance business, the insurance regulatory authority shall shut down such operations, confiscate the illegal income and impose a fine of not less than the amount of and not more than five times the illegal income. If there is no illegal income or if the illegal income is less than RMB 200,000, it shall impose a fine of not less than RMB 200,000 and not more than RMB 1 million.

Article 160 If this Law is violated by establishing a dedicated insurance agency or insurance brokerage without authorization, or by engaging in insurance agency business or insurance brokerage business without a permit to engage in insurance agency business or insurance brokerage business, the insurance regulatory authority shall shut down such operations, confiscate the illegal income and impose a fine of not less than the amount of and not more than five times the illegal income. If there is no illegal income or if the illegal income is less than RMB

50,000, it shall impose a fine of not less than RMB 50,000 and not more than RMB 300,000.

Article 161 If an insurance company violates this Law by operating beyond its approved scope of business, the insurance regulatory authority shall order it to correct the matter within a specified period of time, confiscate its illegal income and impose a fine of not less than the amount of and not more than five times the illegal income; if there is no illegal income or if the illegal income is less than RMB 100,000, it shall impose a fine of not less than RMB 100,000 and not more than RMB 500,000. If it fails to carry out a correction of the matter by the specified period of time or causes serious consequences, the insurance regulatory authority shall order it to suspend operations and undergo rectification, or revoke its business permit.

Article 162 If an insurance company commits any of the acts set forth in Article 116 hereof, the insurance regulatory authority shall order it to correct the matter and impose a fine of not less than RMB 50,000 and not more than RMB 300,000. If the circumstances are serious, the insurance regulatory authority shall place restrictions on its scope of business, order it to cease accepting new business or revoke its business permit.

Article 163 If an insurance company violates Article 84 hereof, the insurance regulatory authority shall order it to correct the matter and impose a fine of not less than RMB 10,000 and not more than RMB 100,000.

Article 164 If an insurance company violates this Law by committing either of the following acts, the insurance regulatory authority shall order it to correct the matter and impose a fine of not less than RMB 50,000 and not more than RMB 300,000:

(1) offering over-insurance in serious circumstances;

(2) insuring a person without capacity for civil acts and stipulating death as a condition for payment of insurance benefits.

Article 165 If this Law is violated by the committing of any of the following acts, the insurance regulatory authority shall order a correction of the matter and impose a fine of not less than RMB 50,000 and not more than RMB 300,000; if the circumstances are serious, the insurance regulatory authority may place restrictions on the scope of business, order cessation of the acceptance of new business, or revoke the business permit:

(1) failure to deposit a security bond in accordance with provisions or use of such security bond in violation of provisions;

(2) failure to allocate or carry over funds to its various liability reserves in accordance with provisions;

(3) failure to make contributions to the insurance security fund or allocations to the common reserve in accordance with provisions;

(4) failure to reinsure an insurance in accordance with provisions;

(5) failure to use insurance company funds in accordance with provisions;

(6) establishment of a (sub-) branch or representative office without approval;

(7) failure to apply for approval of insurance terms and premium rates in accordance with provisions.

Article 166 If an insurance agency or an insurance brokerage commits any of the acts set forth in Article 131 hereof, the insurance regulatory authority shall order it to rectify the matter and impose a fine of not less than RMB 50,000 and not more than RMB 300,000. If the circumstances are serious, the insurance regulatory authority shall revoke its business permit.

Article 167 If an insurance agency or an insurance brokerage violates this Law by committing either of the following acts, the insurance regulatory authority shall order it to correct the matter and impose a fine of not less than RMB 20,000 and not more than RMB 100,000; if the circumstances are serious, the insurance regulatory authority shall order it to suspend operations and undergo rectification or revoke its business permit:

(1) failure to deposit a security bond or take out professional liability insurance in accordance with provisions;

(2) failure, in accordance with regulations, to keep dedicated account books to record its business receipts and expenditures.

Article 168 If a dedicated insurance agency or an insurance brokerage violates this Law by establishing a (sub-) branch or by changing its organizational form without approval, the insurance regulatory authority shall order it to correct the matter and impose a fine of not less than RMB 10,000 and not more than RMB 50,000.

Article 169 If this Law is violated by engaging personnel who do not have the qualifications for their position, or practice qualifications, the insurance regulatory authority shall order a correction of the matter and impose a fine of not less than RMB 20,000 and not more than RMB 100,000.

Article 170 If this Law is violated by transferring, leasing out or lending out a business permit, the insurance regulatory authority shall impose a fine of not less than RMB 10,000 and not more than RMB 100,000. If the circumstances are serious, the insurance regulatory authority shall order a suspension of operations to undergo rectification or revoke the business permit.

Article 171 If this Law is violated by the committing any of the following acts, the insurance regulatory authority shall order a correction of the matter within a specified period of time; and if a correction is not carried out by the specified period of time, it shall impose a fine of not less than RMB 10,000 and not more than RMB 100,000:

(1) failure to submit or keep reports, statements, documents or information in accordance with regulations, or failure to provide relevant information or data in accordance with pro-

visions;

(2) failure to submit insurance terms or premium rates for the record in accordance with provisions;

(3) failure to disclose information in accordance with provisions.

Article 172 If this Law is violated by the committing of any of the following acts, the insurance regulatory authority shall order a correction of the matter and impose a fine of not less than RMB 100,000 and not more than RMB 500,000; if the circumstances are serious, the insurance regulatory authority may place restrictions on the scope of business, order cessation of the acceptance of new business or revoke the business permit:

(1) preparation or provision of fraudulent reports, statements, documents or information;

(2) refusal of, or interference with, a legal monitoring inspection;

(3) failure to use approved or recorded insurance terms or premium rates in accordance with provisions.

Article 173 If an insurance company, insurance asset management company, dedicated insurance agency or insurance brokerage violates this Law, the insurance regulatory authority shall, in addition to imposing penalties thereon in accordance with Articles 161 to 172 hereof as applicable, give its supervisors directly in charge and other directly responsible persons a warning and fine them not less than RMB 10,000 and not more than RMB 100,000; if the circumstances are serious, it shall revoke their qualifications for their positions or their practice qualifications.

Article 174 If an individual insurance agent violates this Law, the insurance regulatory authority shall give him/her a warning and may fine him/her up to RMB 20,000; if the circumstances are serious, it shall fine him/her not less than RMB 20,000 and not more than RMB 100,000 and may revoke his/her qualification certificate.

If a person without lawful qualifications engages in individual insurance agent activities, the insurance regulatory authority shall give him/her a warning and may fine him/her up to RMB 20,000; if the circumstances are serious, it shall fine him not less than RMB 20,000 and not more than RMB 100,000.

Article 175 If a foreign insurance institution establishes a representative office in the People's Republic of China without the approval of the State Council's insurance regulatory authority, the State Council's insurance regulatory authority shall shut it down and impose a fine of not less than RMB 50,000 and not more than RMB 300,000.

If a representative office established in the People's Republic of China by a foreign insurance institution engages in insurance business activities, the insurance regulatory authority shall order a correction of the matter, confiscate the illegal income and impose a fine of not less than the amount of and not more than five times the illegal income; if there is no illegal income or if the illegal income is less than RMB 200,000 it shall impose a fine of not less than RMB 200,000 and not more than RMB 1,000,000. It may order that the chief representative be replaced. If the circumstances are serious, it shall close the office down.

Article 176 If a proposer, the insured or beneficiary commits any of the following acts and the insurance fraud activity engaged in by it/him/her is not sufficient to constitute a criminal offence, it/he/she shall be subjected to administrative penalties in accordance with the law:

(1) the proposer deliberately creates a fictitious subject matter of insurance so as to fraudulently obtain insurance proceeds;

(2) he/she fabricates an insured event that did not occur, or fabricates false reasons for an event or overstates the extent of the loss so as to fraudulently obtain insurance proceeds;

(3) he/she willfully causes an insured event so as to fraudulently obtain insurance proceeds.

If an assessor, appraiser or attester of an insured event deliberately provides false supporting documentation to create the conditions for the proposer, the insured or the beneficiary to commit insurance fraud, it/he/she shall be penalized in accordance with the preceding paragraph.

Article 177 If a third party is caused to incur damage due to a violation of this Law, civil liability shall be borne in accordance with the law.

Article 178 If the lawful exercise by an insurance regulatory authority and its working personnel of their right to conduct a monitoring inspection or investigation in accordance with the law is refused or hindered, public security control penalties shall be imposed if violence or intimidation was not used.

Article 179 If a law or administrative regulation is violated and the circumstances are serious, the State Council's insurance regulatory authority may ban the relevant responsible persons from the insurance industry for a certain period of time up to life.

Article 180 A member of the personnel of an insurance regulatory authority who is involved in oversight work shall be sanctioned in accordance with the law if:

(1) he/she violates regulations in approving the establishment of an organization;

(2) he/she violates regulations in approving insurance terms or insurance premium rates;

(3) he/she violates regulations in conducting an onsite inspection;

(4) he/she violates regulations in checking an account or freezing funds;

(5) he/she divulges trade secrets of a relevant work unit or individual to which he/she is privy;

(6) he/she violates provisions in imposing administrative penalties;

(7) he/she commits another act of abuse of his authority or dereliction of his/her duties.

Article 181　If a violation of this Law constitutes a criminal offence, criminal liability shall be pursued in accordance with the law.

Chapter VIII　Supplementary Provisions

Article 182　An insurance company shall join an insurance association. An insurance agency, insurance brokerage or insurance assessor may join an insurance association.

An insurance association is an organization responsible for the self-regulation of the insurance industry and is an association with legal personality.

Article 183　This Law shall govern the commercial insurance business engaged in by insurance organizations, other than insurance companies, that are established in accordance with the law.

Article 184　Relevant provisions of the PRC Maritime Law shall apply to marine insurance. For matters not covered by the PRC Maritime Law, relevant provisions of this Law shall apply.

Article 185　This Law shall apply to Sino-foreign equity joint insurance companies, wholly foreign-owned insurance companies, and branch companies of foreign insurance companies; however, where other laws or administrative regulations provide otherwise, such provisions shall prevail.

Article 186　The state supports the development of insurance business for agricultural production services. Agricultural insurance shall be separately provided for by laws or administrative regulations. If laws or administrative regulations provide otherwise in respect of mandatory insurance, such provisions shall apply.

Article 187　This Law shall be effective as of October 1, 2009.

國家圖書館出版品預行編目(CIP)資料

新編保險英語 / 袁建華 編著. -- 第一版.
-- 臺北市 : 財經錢線文化出版 : 崧博發行, 2018.12
　面 ; 　公分

ISBN 978-957-680-282-9(平裝)

1.英語 2.保險學 3.讀本

805.18　　　　107019507

書　名：新編保險英語
作　者：袁建華 編著
發行人：黃振庭
出版者：財經錢線文化事業有限公司
發行者：崧博出版事業有限公司
E-mail：sonbookservice@gmail.com
粉絲頁　　　　　網　址
地　址：台北市中正區延平南路六十一號五樓一室
8F.-815, No.61, Sec. 1, Chongqing S. Rd., Zhongzheng Dist., Taipei City 100, Taiwan (R.O.C.)
電　話：(02)2370-3310　傳　真：(02) 2370-3210
總經銷：紅螞蟻圖書有限公司
地　址：台北市內湖區舊宗路二段 121 巷 19 號
電　話:02-2795-3656　傳真:02-2795-4100　網址：
印　刷 ：京峯彩色印刷有限公司（京峰數位）

　　本書版權為西南財經大學出版社所有授權崧博出版事業有限公司獨家發行電子書及繁體書繁體版。若有其他相關權利及授權需求請與本公司聯繫。

定價：400元

發行日期：2018 年 12 月第一版

◎ 本書以POD印製發行